Disney

Pirates of the Caribbean

THE CURSE OF THE BLACK PEARL

Adapted by Elizabeth Rudnick

Based on the screenplay written by
Ted Elliott & Terry Rossio and
Screen story by Ted Elliott & Terry Rossio
and Stuart Beattie and Jay Wolpert
Based on Walt Disney's Pirates of the Caribbean
Produced by Jerry Bruckheimer
Directed by Gore Verbinski

Disney PRESS
New York

For information address Disney Press, 114 Fifth Avenue, New York, New York 10011-5690.
Printed in the United States of America
Second Edition
1 3 5 7 9 10 8 6 4 2
This book is set in 13-point Charlotte Book.
Library of Congress Control Number: 2006933207
ISBN-13: 978-1-4231-0710-1
ISBN-10: 1-4231-0710-1
Visit DisneyPirates.Com

Chapter 1

Young Elizabeth Swann stood at the bow of the HMS *Dauntless*, one hand resting on the rail as she sang an old pirate shanty. The *Dauntless* was one of the strongest ships in the Royal Navy. The ship was agile and fast and, for those reasons, she had been commandeered to carry Elizabeth and her father to Port Royal, where Elizabeth's father was governor.

The sailing had been smooth and clear for most of the journey. But now, a thick fog blanketed the unusually calm sea, obscuring the *Dauntless*'s bowsprit and masts. As the wind whipped Elizabeth's light brown hair around her fair face, she continued to sing her shanty. She was unbothered, perhaps even entranced, by the eerie calm of the Caribbean Sea.

Suddenly, a hand clamped down on her shoulder. Startled, she quickly turned and found herself face-to-face with a member of the crew—

one Mr. Joshamee Gibbs. He was an older man whose appearance seemed like a record of all the places he'd sailed to and the things he'd done and seen. His face was wrinkled and weather worn and his hair was as gray as a stormy sea. As he leaned close to Elizabeth, she could smell the strong scent of the sea on his skin and clothes. "Quiet, missy!" he snarled. Then lowering his own voice, he added, "Cursed pirates sail these waters. You want to call 'em down on us?"

Elizabeth opened her mouth to respond, but before she could, a commanding voice called out. "Mr. Gibbs. That will do."

Striding over to Elizabeth and Mr. Gibbs, Lieutenant Norrington came to a stop and glared down at the older seaman. Outfitted in the uniform of the Royal Navy with a wig of shocking white hair below his hat, Norrington cut a striking figure. He had been ordered to accompany Governor Swann and his daughter to Port Royal. And to Norrington, that duty included keeping old, superstitious sailors away from his young charge.

Following close behind Norrington was Governor Weatherby Swann—Elizabeth's father. He wore the white, curly wig of a political figure and while he looked uneasy aboard the swaying ship, he still carried himself as befit his high status. But, the presence of neither Norrington nor the governor was enough to stop Gibbs from speaking his mind.

"She was singing about pirates," he argued. "Bad luck to sing about pirates, with us mired in this unnatural fog—mark my words."

"Consider them marked," Norrington responded in his clipped British accent. "Now, on your way." He continued to glare at Gibbs, waiting for the sailor to leave.

Finally, Gibbs shrugged and turned to go, but not before muttering, "Bad luck to have a woman onboard. Even a miniature one."

Elizabeth didn't seem to notice the remark. Her mind was still reeling from what Gibbs had said earlier. Cursed pirates roamed these waters!

"I think it would be rather exciting to meet a pirate," she said dreamily.

"Think again, Miss Swann," Norrington replied pointedly. "Vile and dissolute creatures, the lot of them."

From his spot beside the lieutenant, Governor Swann sighed. How was Elizabeth to be a proper member of Port Royal society if she remained obsessed with pirates and legends of the sea? "Elizabeth," he said, "wouldn't it be wonderful if we comport ourselves as befits our class and station?"

"Yes, father," she replied dutifully. But as she turned back to gaze over the bow's rail and out to sea, she added, "But I *still* think it would be exciting to meet a pirate. . . ."

Her voice broke off as she imagined what it would be like. Would he be kind? Most undoubtedly not. In all likelihood, he would be mysterious, and threatening, and . . .

Suddenly, Elizabeth was distracted by a movement through the fog. Something appeared to be floating out on the water. The shadow was faint and seemed to sway back and forth along the top of the waves—almost as if it were dancing on the swells. Slowly, it came closer. Elizabeth noticed a spot of color, and as it finally broke free of the mist, she gasped. It was a parasol! Elizabeth watched as it slowly came closer and closer, drifting toward the *Dauntless* before gently bumping into the hull.

Elizabeth could not believe her eyes. A

parasol in the middle of the sea? It just did not seem right. As she gazed down at the fragile item, another, much larger, item floated into view. It looked like something heavy and lifeless lying on top of a large piece of flotsam. Elizabeth leaned over the rail and squinted to get a closer look. Then she realized just what it was.

"Look!" she cried. "There's a boy in the water!"

Elizabeth's cries brought Norrington, her father, and most of the crew running to the rail. Murmurs and shouts rose up as they caught sight of the boy lying on his back on a small piece of wreckage. "Fetch a hook—haul him out of there," Norrington ordered.

The sailors, who had been looking overboard, leaped into action. Swinging one of the *Dauntless*'s hooks out over the rail, they lowered it down and quickly hauled the unconscious boy aboard. When he was safely on deck, Norrington leaned over to examine him. "He's still breathing," the captain declared.

"Where did he come from?" Governor Swann asked.

A gasp from Gibbs prevented Norrington

from responding. "Mother of all that's holy . . ." Gibbs muttered, staring into the fog.

All hands on deck, including young Elizabeth, turned and followed Gibbs's gaze out to the sea. It was no longer empty. Where moments before there had been nothing but rolling waves and endless fog, a burning hull now floated. As the *Dauntless* sailed past, they could make out the remains of the ship's cargo. Broken crates, splintered wood, and wardrobes' worth of clothing littered the waves.

Gibbs spoke up again, his mind still on Elizabeth's ill-timed song. "Everyone's thinking it! Pirates!"

Norrington shot Gibbs a stern glare. Then, Norrington ordered the crew to search for survivors. If the boy had made it, there was a chance others had as well. While the sailors rushed about, Governor Swann stepped away from the rail and made his way to Elizabeth's side. His daughter was kneeling beside the boy, a concerned look creasing her brow.

"Elizabeth, the boy is in your charge now. You'll watch over him?" Governor Swann asked.

Elizabeth nodded and returned her attention to the boy. Since they had pulled him onto the *Dauntless*, he had not moved. His breathing was shallow and his skin pale and waterlogged. But it was the look in his eyes when they fluttered open that was the most haunting. He seemed so sad and lost. She brushed a lock of brown hair from his forehead, desperate to find out what had happened.

"My name is Elizabeth Swann," she said, placing his hand in hers.

With a cough, the boy tried to speak, and finally he managed. "Will Turner."

Will slipped back into unconsciousness, but before he did, his body shifted in such a way that the collar of his shirt opened. There, attached to a chain and resting on his bare neck, was a gold medallion. Curious, Elizabeth tugged it free. What she saw made her eyes grow wide. Staring back at her, engraved on the face of the Medallion, was a skull. Elizabeth came to a quick conclusion. Will must be a pirate!

Hastily, Elizabeth hid the Medallion under her coat. She couldn't let the lieutenant and her father see it. If they did, Will's life would most certainly be in danger.

Norrington then appeared at her side again. "Did he speak?"

"His name is Will Turner," Elizabeth replied. "That's all I found out."

Nodding in approval, Norrington moved on and Elizabeth let out a sigh of relief. When she was sure that the lieutenant was not coming back, Elizabeth pulled the Medallion out of her coat. But before she could take a closer look, she caught movement out of the corner of her eye. Looking up, she nearly gasped. There, moving silently through the thick fog, was a tall ship with black sails. At the top of its highest mast flew a flag—a flag that had the same skull as on the Medallion. A pirate ship!

Then, as silently as it had appeared, the ship slipped quickly back into the fog. On the deck of the *Dauntless*, Elizabeth watched until all she could see was the black-and-white flag billowing in the wind.

Elizabeth Swann awoke with a start. The deck of the *Dauntless* was gone, replaced by the safety of her room in the governor's mansion. She had been dreaming again of Will and the pirate ship that she had seen eight years earlier on her way here, to Port Royal. And as always, the dream was so vivid and real to her. Her heart still racing, she reached over and turned up the oil lamp that rested beside her canopied bed. The room filled with dim light, gently illuminating the lavish furnishings and artwork that signified Elizabeth's status as the governor's daughter. Easing out of bed, Elizabeth picked up her oil lamp and made her way to her dressing table. She pulled open the top drawer and reached inside.

Her hand closed around a familiar object. Pulling her hand back out, she looked down into her open palm. There, lying faceup, was the gold

Medallion she had taken from Will's neck eight years ago. The grinning skull hauntingly stared at her.

A loud knock on the door caused Elizabeth to jump.

"Elizabeth," came her father's voice. "Is everything all right? Are you decent?"

"Yes . . . yes," Elizabeth stammered as the doorknob began to turn. She quickly placed the Medallion around her neck and threw on a dressing gown, just as her father walked into the room carrying a large box. Estrella, Elizabeth's maid, followed and began to pull back the heavy curtains. Sunlight flooded the room. Outside, the town of Port Royal bustled alongside the blue waters of the Caribbean. Sitting out on a bluff was Fort Charles, its men, armed with cannons, keeping watch over the harbor.

Governor Swann smiled at his daughter. "I have a gift for you," he said proudly, holding the box out to her. Before she could respond, her father opened the box to reveal an elegant gown.

Elizabeth let out a pleased gasp. "May I inquire as to the occasion?" She asked taking the dress behind a screen as her father paced the room.

"I did think you could wear it to the ceremony today," he replied cautiously.

From behind the screen, Elizabeth silently groaned. The promotion ceremony! Of course! Since Norrington had accompanied Elizabeth and her father to Port Royal, he had only grown in standing with the Royal Navy. Now he was being made a commodore. Elizabeth knew her father would like nothing more than to see his only daughter wedded to such a noble man.

As if reading her mind, her father continued. "Captain Norrington, or, rather, Commodore Norrington . . . a fine gentleman. He fancies you, you know." Pausing, he added, "How's it coming?"

In reply, Elizabeth let out a gasp. Behind the screen, Estrella was pulling the laces on the corset as tight as they would go. Elizabeth felt the air being pushed out of her lungs as her ribs were bound tightly in the whalebone contraption. While the dress was beautiful—full of frill and lace—it was lacking in comfort.

"I'm told that dress is the very latest fashion in London," her father said.

"Women in London must have learned to not breathe," Elizabeth replied. She was not looking forward to being paraded around in front of the newly named Commodore Norrington in such a dress. Trying to take a deep breath, she winced. Deep breathing was clearly out of the question.

A moment later, the fitting was interrupted by a servant who announced a visitor.

Excusing himself, Governor Swann headed downstairs. Shortly after, Elizabeth followed, a frown on her face, as she tried to figure out a way to breathe in the tight corset and walk at the same time. At the top of the stairs she caught sight of the visitor and her frown disappeared, replaced by a beaming smile.

"Mr. Turner!" the governor exclaimed from below.

Will Turner stood in the foyer of the governor's mansion, one hand clutching a long, rectangular case, the other behind his back. His black coat was worn and in need of darning, and his boots were scuffed. But Elizabeth did not mind. The frightened boy she had rescued eight years before was gone, replaced by a handsome young man. From the top of the stairs, out of sight of her father and Will, Elizabeth stared unabashedly at his sad eyes, strong jaw, and thick brown hair, which was pulled back into a ponytail.

"Good day, sir," Will replied, unaware of Elizabeth's eavesdropping. "I have your order." Walking over to a table in the foyer, Will placed the case gently on top. Then, with the utmost reverence, he opened it to reveal a dress sword and scabbard. Will waited as Governor Swann pulled the sword from the case before continuing. "The blade is foiled steel. That's gold filigree laid into the handle. If I may . . ." Taking the sword back, he continued to point out its strengths.

"Very impressive," Governor Swann said when Will was done. "Do pass my compliments on to your master."

Sighing, Will nodded. The "master" was actually none other than Will himself. But the old blacksmith Will worked for tended to take all the credit for Will's skill.

"I shall," Will said politely. "A craftsman is always pleased to hear his work is appreciated . . ." His voice broke off.

Elizabeth was walking down the stairs, a smile on her lips. Her hair gleamed in the fractured sunlight and Will took an involuntary step forward.

"Elizabeth! You look stunning," her father said, voicing Will's thoughts.

But Elizabeth did not seem to notice her father or his compliments. Her eyes were riveted to the young swordsmith standing beside him.

"Will! It's so good to see you," she said warmly. "I dreamt about you last night. About the day we met. Do you remember?"

"I could never forget it, Miss Swann."

Oblivious to the effect she had on him, Elizabeth pressed on. "Will, how many times must I ask you to call me Elizabeth?"

"Once more, Miss Swann," he said. "As always."

Elizabeth's face fell. Will was just too proper and polite. Straightening her back and holding her head high, she descended the rest of the stairs. Right before she walked out the door, she turned. "Good day, *Mr.* Turner," she said coolly.

Without another word, she walked out the door and into her carriage, leaving Will Turner behind.

Inside the carriage, Elizabeth Swann sat in stormy silence. Will Turner was so aggravating! To act so proper and poised. How could he do it? Did he not want to smile? To joke with her as they once had?

The carriage made its way into Port Royal and toward Fort Charles, where Norrington's ceremony was to take place. But Elizabeth did not notice the beautiful sea or the bustling town. Her mind was still back in the foyer.

From his seat opposite hers in the carriage, Governor Swann spoke.

"Dear," he said, "I do hope you demonstrate a bit more decorum in front of Commodore Norrington. It is only through his efforts that Port Royal has become at all civilized."

Elizabeth did not reply. Instead, she turned and stared out at the sea. She wished she were free of this life and its "decorum." Free to sail away and not look back.

Meanwhile, at that moment, unseen by Elizabeth Swann or her father, a man who was already free sailed into Port Royal. Though perhaps "sailed" was not the most accurate of terms.

Standing atop the yardarm of a small fishing dory named the *Jolly Mon*, Captain Jack Sparrow surveyed the town of Port Royal. His tricornered hat sat jauntily atop his head, revealing the hint of a red bandanna beneath. When he smiled, the sun glinted off his several gold teeth. On almost every one of his fingers flashed a ring, and bits of silver and other trinkets hung from his brown, dreadlocked hair.

Looking down, Jack noticed that the *Jolly Mon* was no longer sailing on top of the water so much as through it. The boat was sinking.

Jack jumped from the yardarm to the deck and felt water soak into his knee-high boots. The deck was overrun with water. Quickly, he searched through the deck's clutter and found a bucket. Picking it up, he began to bail.

While Jack bailed, the *Jolly Mon* continued to sail into Port Royal's harbor. Quietly it slipped by a rocky outcropping from which five skeletons hung from nooses. One wore a sign that read: PIRATES—BE YE WARNED. Pausing, Jack Sparrow took off his hat and placed it above his heart—a moment of exaggerated respect for the doomed pirates.

The harbor of Port Royal was crowded with boats. There were fishing vessels of all sizes, but the most impressive was the HMS *Dauntless*, which lay at anchor in the tranquil waters. Her fifty cannons were quiet, but even at peace, she was an imposing vessel. Jack Sparrow took his time surveying the *Dauntless* before his eye was caught by a smaller vessel—the HMS *Interceptor*. The *Interceptor* was nowhere near the size of the *Dauntless*, but she was sleek and speedy. Glancing at the ship, Jack Sparrow's eyes sparked, but then he turned and focused on the task at hand—namely, docking.

Unfortunately, docking was going to be difficult, as the *Jolly Mon* was now almost completely underwater. Only the small portion of the mast and yardarm Jack had climbed back up on remained above water. With comic precision, Jack reached the dock just as the tip of the mast completely disappeared beneath the water. Stepping onto the dock, he came face-to-face with a very confused harbormaster.

"Hold up there, ye!" the harbormaster shouted. "It's a shilling to tie up your boat."

Jack glanced at him quizzically and then looked over his shoulder at the now fully submerged *Jolly Mon.* Not bothering to answer the harbormaster, Jack shrugged and attempted to move on.

But the harbormaster would not let him pass. "Rules are rules. And, I'll need to know your name."

A young boy who had been following the harbormaster opened up a ledger. Looking at it, Jack pulled out a coin purse and threw a few coins onto the open book.

"What do you say to three shillings, and we *forget* the name?" Jack asked.

For a moment, the harbormaster just stared at Jack, a mixture of disbelief and annoyance etched on his face. Then, thinking better of it, he closed the ledger. "Welcome to Port Royal . . . *Mr. Smith.*"

High above the harbor, inside the walls of Fort

Charles, Norrington stood at attention. He was dressed in the uniform of a commodore of the Royal Navy, and looked every bit the nautical hero he was. Standing before him was Governor Swann. With choreographed precision, Swann presented the sword and scabbard Will Turner had delivered earlier to the newly appointed commodore.

With a swish of the sword, *Commodore* Norrington saluted the governor before turning to his officers and the rest of the crowd that had assembled for the ceremony.

Meanwhile, Elizabeth Swann struggled to breathe. With every breath she took, the corset seemed to tighten around her ribs. The fan she held in her hand whipped back and forth as she tried to stay upright. In front of her, Norrington continued to preen, clearly enjoying his moment. As for Elizabeth? She did not know how much longer she could remain standing.

Back at the docks, Jack Sparrow was having no trouble breathing. In fact, everything seemed to be slipping into place perfectly. After disembarking from the *Jolly Mon*, he headed toward the navy dock. There, the *Interceptor* was anchored in all her beauty. Guarding her berth were two of the Royal Navy's dimmest marines—Murtogg and Mullroy. The two men wore the uniform of the navy, but instead of helping the duo command respect, their clothes somehow made them seem comical. Their bumbling personalities were not suited for such official attire. Murtogg's belly strained at his coat, and Mullroy's white pants seemed a bit too baggy for him. While the officers were up at Fort Charles watching Norrington's promotion to commodore, Murtogg and Mullroy had been assigned to guard the *Interceptor*.

As he swayed over to the marines, Jack Sparrow took in everything—from the *Interceptor*'s hull to the blank expression on the men's faces. Taking the *Interceptor* was going to be easier than he had hoped.

"This dock is off-limits to civilians," Murtogg said as soon as Jack walked up.

"Didn't know," Jack said, as the sound of drums and trumpets drifted down from the fort above. "Some sort of high-toned and fancy affair up at the fort? How could it be that your good selves did not rate an invitation?"

Murtogg glared at the poorly dressed stranger. "*Someone* has to make sure this dock stays off-limits to civilians," he explained.

Jack paused and looked past the guards at the *Interceptor*. Swaying slightly, he reached out to run his fingers along her sides. "This must be some important boat," he said casually. While he was well aware of nautical terminology, it behooved him to play dumb. And playing dumb with two nitwits was quite an enjoyable game.

At the word "boat," Mullroy rolled his eyes. Clearly they were dealing with a silly civilian who did not know the bow from the stern. "Ship," he pointed out. Then he proudly added, "Commodore Norrington's made it his flagship. He'll use it to hunt down the last dregs of piracy on the Spanish Main."

Jack reached up and played with the goatee that hung from his chin. It was a habit of his from long days at sea. Twisting it around, he waited a moment before responding.

"It seems to me a ship like that," Jack said, turning to motion toward the *Dauntless*, "makes this one here a wee superfluous."

"Oh, the *Dauntless* is the power in these

waters, true enough—but there's no ship as can match the *Interceptor* for speed," Murtogg pointed out, sounding pleased to know so much about his navy's ships.

"That so," Jack said, once again looking thoughtfully at the *Interceptor*. "I've heard of one, supposed to be fast, nigh uncatchable . . . the *Black Pearl*?"

Mullroy let out a laugh. The *Black Pearl* was a legend, an old ghost story told to young children to scare them. Even Mullroy knew not to be afraid of a ship that no one had ever seen—no less sailed on. This wobbling man with the bad teeth and a worn-out jacket was clearly not thinking straight. Mullroy pushed aside any thoughts that the man might be a threat and amended his original comment, "There's no *real* ship as can match the *Interceptor*."

"The *Black Pearl* is a real ship," argued Murtogg. "I've seen it."

Mullroy rolled his eyes. Now even his fellow marine was going loopy. The pair continued to argue back and forth, each one convinced the other was wrong. "You've seen a ship with black sails that's crewed by the damned and captained by a man so evil that hell itself spat him back out?" Mullroy asked as the argument continued to rage.

Murtogg looked down at his boots and shook his head no. Turning to tell Jack, that he was right, there was no ship that could beat the *Interceptor*, Mullroy gasped. Jack was gone!

While the two had been arguing about the evidence for the existence—or lack thereof—of a ship with black sails, Jack had casually sauntered aboard the *Interceptor*. He now stood at the wheel of the ship, examining the compass and other instruments necessary for sailing the vessel. Hearing the marines approach, Jack glanced over at them, feigning surprise.

"Get away from there!" Mullroy shouted. "You don't have permission to be aboard."

"I'm sorry," Jack said innocently as the two ran up the gangplank and boarded the deck. "It's just such a pretty boat . . . ship."

Murtogg and Mullroy had had enough.

"What's your name?" Murtogg demanded.

"Smith. Or Smitty if you like," Jack answered.

"What's your business in Port Royal, Mr. Smith?" Mullroy asked.

"And no lies!" Murtogg added.

Jack smiled. If it was truth this bumbling duo wanted, it was truth he would give them. "I confess: I intend to commandeer one of these ships, pick up a crew in Tortuga, and do a little honest pirating."

Standing aboard the *Interceptor*, Murtogg and Mullroy exchanged confused glances. But they were prevented from any further discussion of Jack's plans for any ships by a commotion from above. Looking up, the three men watched as a young woman teetered on the edge of Fort Charles's imposing wall. For a moment, it appeared she would be fine. But suddenly, her arms flew up and she fell, hitting the water below with a mighty splash.

Moments before Jack Sparrow and his dimwitted foes had witnessed the woman falling from the fort, Commodore Norrington's ceremony had come to an end. Norrington fought his way through the crowd that had gathered, making his way to Elizabeth Swann's side. In the afternoon light, she looked angelic. Her face was pale, and her eyelashes fluttered as he gently guided her away from the crowd and came to a stop along the cliff wall.

"This promotion confirms that I have accomplished the goals I set for myself," Norrington began.

Elizabeth strained to pay attention as Norrington spoke, but she found it difficult. Standing in the hot sun throughout the ceremony had caused her to feel faint, and trying to breathe in her new dress and corset was impossible. Every breath she took felt too short, and her vision began to grow blurry.

Unaware of the distress Elizabeth was under, Norrington continued. "But the promotion also casts into sharp relief that which I have not achieved: marriage to a fine woman." He paused before adding, "You have become a fine woman, Elizabeth."

The tightness in Elizabeth's chest grew as Norrington's words sank in. Clutching at her chest, she exclaimed, "I can't breathe." Then, suddenly, she fainted, tumbling over the wall of the fort . . . and into thin air. Norrington watched in horror as she vanished into the water below. With a cry, he turned and ran, heading to the harbor. . . .

"Aren't you going to save her?" Jack asked the two marines.

"I can't swim," Mullroy replied while Murtogg shook his head. He couldn't swim either.

"Prides of the king's navy, you are," Jack said, lacing his voice with a heavy dose of sarcasm. Sighing, he began to take off his coat. It looked like he would have to wait to steal the *Interceptor* until after he saved the lassie. Next, he took off his pistol, followed by his bandolier, which jingled with trinkets, and finally, he pulled off his hat. Ceremoniously, he handed them to Murtogg. "Don't lose those," he said, and without another word, he turned and dove into the water.

As Elizabeth drifted toward the sea floor, the Medallion that she still wore around her neck floated up. Suddenly, a shaft of light slanted through the water, illuminating the Medallion. Back on shore, Murtogg and Mullroy felt the dock beneath their feet pulse as if hit by a mighty wave. As the wind picked up and the sky clouded over, they moved closer together.

Meanwhile, underneath the water, Jack swam toward Elizabeth, unaware of the shock on shore or the odd change in the air. Reaching her, Jack wrapped his arm around her waist and began to head for the surface. He took several strokes before realizing he was not moving fast enough. The dress was pulling both of them down. Quickly, he reached around to the back of the flimsy material and ripped it off her. As it came free of her body, it caught in the current and slowly began to sink back to the floor. Jack quickly swam Elizabeth to the dock.

Murtogg and Mullroy, still slightly shaky, helped haul Elizabeth out of the water. When she was safe, Jack pulled himself up onto the dock.

More interested in getting his own breath back, Jack ignored the young woman who now lay before him. But Mullroy leaned over and put his cheek against her nose and mouth. "She's not breathing," he said.

Jack sighed. Did he have to do *everything*? Stepping forward, he deftly snatched a knife from Murtogg's belt and knelt down beside Elizabeth. In one quick and well-practiced move, he ran the knife down her corset, tearing it in two. For a moment, nothing happened. Then, Elizabeth, finally freed from the confines of the corset, began to cough and sputter. She was breathing!

"I never would have thought of that," Mullroy said in awe.

Jack smiled. "Clearly, you've never been to Singapore," he said mysteriously. But before he could elaborate, his attention was caught by the Medallion around Elizabeth's neck. Reaching down, Jack picked it up and turned it over in his hand.

He was still kneeling at Elizabeth's side when a shadow fell across him, followed by the cold touch of steel against his neck.

"On your feet," a voice ordered.

Slowly, Jack stood. The scene did not bode well for him. The young woman lay across the deck, her corset ripped in half, and her dress gone. Meanwhile, he stood there without his sword, hat, or gun . . . defenseless against the man standing before him.

"Shoot that man!" Norrington cried out, pointing his sword at Jack.

Jack looked over at Elizabeth who was now being tended to by the very nervous governor.

"Father!" Elizabeth cried. "Commodore. Surely, you don't intend to kill my rescucr?"

Norrington looked down his sword at Jack. Then, ever so slowly, he pulled the sword away from Jack's neck and placed it back in its sheath. With a reluctant sigh, he held out his hand. "I believe thanks are in order," he said.

Gingerly, Jack reached out his hand and began to shake with Norrington. But in one quick move, the commodore tightened his grip and with his other hand yanked Jack's sleeve back. There, for all to see, was the letter *P* branded on Jack's arm.

"Had a brushup with the East India Trading Company—pirate?" Norrington asked. The men who had followed the commodore from Fort Charles drew their pistols.

As Norrington looked down on the pirate brand, his eyes caught sight of something else. There, right below the *P*, was a tattoo of a small bird flying across the ocean. It was faded and worn, but it told Norrington exactly what he needed to know. "Well, well . . . Jack Sparrow, isn't it?"

Jack grimaced. "*Captain* Jack Sparrow. If you please," he said, dropping into an elaborate bow.

"I don't see your ship—*Captain*," Norrington sneered.

Murtogg and Mullroy looked at each other. They had been keeping quiet to avoid any questions as to why they let a *pirate* save the governor's daughter. Murtogg finally spoke up. "He said he'd come to commandeer one."

"These are his, sir," added Mullroy, showing the pistol and bandolier.

Jack remained quiet as Norrington took the items from Mullroy and began to examine them. He peered into the gun and examined the belt, pulling trinkets off as he went—including a compass that dangled from the belt. When he had finished, he looked at Jack and smiled.

"No additional shot nor powder," Norrington began. Then, holding up Jack's Compass, he added, "It doesn't bear true." Lastly, he pulled the sword from its scabbard. Laughing at the pirate's obvious misfortune, he sheathed the sword. "You are, without a doubt, the worst pirate I have ever heard of," he stated in conclusion.

"Ah, but you *have* heard of me," Jack replied.

Norrington signaled one of his lieutenants to shackle Jack Sparrow. But before the man could get close, Elizabeth stepped forward. The jacket that had been covering her slipped off her shoulders, but she did not seem to care. Her attention was focused solely on the events unfolding in front of her.

"Commodore," she stated, "I must protest. Pirate or not, this man saved my life."

"One good deed is not enough to redeem a man for a lifetime of wickedness," Norrington replied evenly, trying to keep the frustration from his voice. Elizabeth seemed far too concerned with the safety of this *pirate.*

With another nod to the lieutenants, Jack was quickly shackled. The pirate safely captured, the rest of the men stood down, placing their weapons back in their belts. Only one marine continued to hold his pistol. That was just what Jack wanted to see. Before anyone knew what was happening, Jack snapped the corset that he still held in his hand around the wrist of the marine with the pistol. Flinging the man's hand into the air, Jack dislodged the pistol and sent it sailing smoothly out into the water.

As everyone turned to watch the gun fall, Jack sidestepped across the dock and grabbed Elizabeth. Throwing his manacled hands around her neck, he pulled her back against him.

Too late, the rest of Norrington's men drew their weapons. But now Jack had the perfect shield—Elizabeth. "Commodore Norrington . . . my pistol and belt, please," he said with a smug smile upon his lips. When Norrington hesitated, Jack pulled the manacles tighter against Elizabeth's neck, causing her to squirm. Norrington grabbed the pistol and belt from Murtogg and held them out. But Jack was not to be fooled. If he released Elizabeth to retrieve the items, his shield would be gone.

"Elizabeth—it is Elizabeth?" Jack whispered into his captive's ear.

Fuming, Elizabeth struggled against Jack's arms, trying to get as far from him as possible. But he simply pulled the manacles tighter and brought her closer. "Miss Swann," she replied.

"Miss Swann, if you'll be so kind?" Jack asked. Leaning forward, Elizabeth took the pistol and belt from Norrington. Before she knew what was happening, Jack had grabbed the pistol and now held it against her temple. With her firmly in his grasp, Jack pulled her around so that they were face-to-face. As he got her to slip his bandolier back on, he smiled deviously.

"You are despicable," she announced.

"I saved your life; now you've saved mine. We're square," he said. Then turning back to Norrington, the governor, and the marines who had gathered, he smiled.

"Gentleman . . . milady . . . you will always remember this as the day you *almost* caught Captain Jack Sparrow."

Shoving Elizabeth away, he turned and grabbed a rope that hung from a nearby scaffold. With one quick movement, he pulled the pin that held the rope in place and shot up toward a higher dock. Below him, the marines opened fire but only Norrington's shot flew true. It hit the rope Jack was hanging on and he began to fall. But the manacles Jack was still wearing on his hands caught on yet another rope, and he quickly slid down it, landing safely on the deck of a docked ship. In an instant, Jack disappeared among the crowds of Port Royal.

As Norrington and the others took off after Captain Jack Sparrow, a breeze began to blow. Standing on the docks with her father, Elizabeth shivered and looked out to sea. On the edge of the harbor, a thick and eerie fog made its way toward the town. Drawing her jacket closer, Elizabeth turned and headed to the safety of her home.

Chapter 5

The fog crept along the streets and alleyways of Port Royal, draping everything in shadow. Combing the side streets and hidden corners, an armed party of marines searched for Captain Jack Sparrow.

Hearing their footsteps fade into the fog, the infamous pirate stepped out from his hiding place in the shadows. Once again, Jack Sparrow had slipped through the fingers of the enemy. Noticing a shop across the way, Jack walked over and tried the doors. They had been left unlocked. With one last look over his shoulder, Jack went in.

Inside, he found himself in a blacksmith's shop. The light was dim, and dust from the floor filtered through the air. Tools of the trade hung from the walls, and yoked to the bellows stood an old donkey that seemed unconcerned with the visitor. Jack smiled. Fortune was on his side today.

Surely among all these tools, there would be something strong enough to cut the manacles from his wrists.

Suddenly, a loud snort sounded throughout the forge and Jack jumped. He was not alone. Glancing around, his eyes came to rest on a bear of a man, slumped over in a chair, an empty bottle cradled in his arms. From the looks of him, Jack assumed this was the blacksmith himself. Given the man's condition, Jack did not think him a threat, and shrugging, he resumed his search for something he could use to take the manacles off. Walking over to the furnace, which was still glowing hot, Jack pulled a short-handled sledge from the wall and held it in his left hand. Then, Jack took a deep breath and reached out his right hand—directly over the furnace. Sweating, Jack waited as long as he could before pulling his hand away and wrapping the glowing chain around a nearby anvil. Then, with a mighty grunt, he brought the sledge down on the chain, shattering it.

One hand unmanacled, he placed it in a bucket of water, watching as the steam bubbled up. To be a pirate was dangerous work, he mused.

But at least he was that much closer to freedom. Hearing someone at the door, he ducked for cover and waited to see who it was.

Will Turner entered the blacksmith shop, still upset over his earlier encounter with Miss Swann. The shop, owned by his employer, Mr. Brown, looked as it had when he left it. Mr. Brown was slumped in a corner, and the tools were all as they should be—all but one. The sledge that usually resided on the wall was now lying on the floor. Walking over, Will leaned down to pick it up when suddenly, the flat side of a sword slapped his hand. Looking up, he found himself face-to-face with a rather unusual-looking man.

Will stared with wide eyes at his attacker. The man's hat sat atop dirty dreads, and his teeth gleamed with gold. And while his clothes could have belonged to any poor sailor, the manacle dangling from his wrist gave him away. "You're the one they're hunting," he said. Then with a sneer, he added, "The *pirate*."

With a tip of his hat, Jack acknowledged Will's statement. From his vantage point, the boy did not seem a threat. He was of slim build, and while his hands appeared strong—most likely from working with hot metal and other tools of the blacksmith trade—his eyes were innocent. Jack very much doubted the boy had ever been in a real fight. But still, something nagged at Jack. "You seem somewhat familiar. Have I threatened you before?"

Will's glare grew darker. "I make it a point to avoid familiarity with pirates," he answered.

"Ah. Then it would be a shame to put a black mark on your record," Jack said, hoping that his escape from Port Royal would remain unhindered. "So, if you'll excuse me . . ." Slowly, he began to back away from Will, heading for the door.

But Will was not as unschooled in the world of fighting as he appeared. In one quick move, he reached over to a nearby grindstone and grabbed a sword resting on top of it. Jumping up and out of the way of Jack's blade, Will swished the sword in one well-practiced motion.

In response, Jack raised his own sword and settled into a fighting stance. If it was a fight this boy wanted, it was a fight he would give him. With a swish of swords, the two began parrying back and forth across the floor of the shop, Jack doing his best to stay one step ahead of the young blacksmith. But it was difficult.

"You know what you're doing," Jack said between thrusts, "I'll give you that."

In response, Will increased the speed of his swipes, matching every step Jack made. He was not going to allow the pirate to go without a fight. For another moment, the fighting remained intense as the pair dueled. But then, suddenly, Jack turned and fled toward the door. Seeing the pirate on the run, Will did the first thing that came to mind. With a grunt, he threw the sword—directly at the door through which Jack was hoping to escape. The sword buried deep into the wood, right above the latch. Reaching the door a moment later, Jack frantically lifted the latch up and down. But it did no good. The sword was stuck in deep and had effectively locked the door!

"That's a good trick," Jack admitted. "Except now, you have no weapon."

Will did not bother to answer. Instead, with a sly smile he simply picked up a sword whose tip had been resting in the furnace. In the bright glow of the sword, Jack's face paled. This boy would not give up, and it was growing tiresome. Sighing, Jack once again began to parry with Will. As their swords continued to clash, Jack looked around, hoping for something to help him out of the current situation. Glancing down, he saw his manacled hand, the chain still dangling from his wrist. Swinging his arm, he attempted to hit Will, but the boy ducked. Jack swung again, and this time the chain made contact with Will's sword, hitting it and sending it flying.

Unfortunately for Jack, another sword lay at the ready and Will quickly grabbed it. Jack groaned. There were far too many weapons in this room. "Who makes all these?" Jack asked as they continued to duel.

"I do," Will answered. "And I practice with them at least three hours a day."

"You need to find yourself a girl," Jack teased. Noticing Will's jaw clench at the mention of "girl," he added, "Or maybe the reason you practice three hours a day is you've found one—but can't get her?"

With a groan of rage, Will kicked out, knocking a rack of swords to the ground. One of them fell into his left hand. He was now doubly armed against the pirate. Swinging wildly, the two continued to fight, their actions taking them onto a long, wooden platform. One end of the platform rested on the ground, while the other was balanced on a barrel. As the pair moved on to it, the wood began to tilt on the barrel like a see-saw. In the heat of the battle, Jack's chain wrapped around Will's sword. Seeing his chance, Will raised his sword up, bedding it deep in the rafter above, and he fastened Jack there, leaving him to dangle.

But Jack was not done fighting. In one swift move, he pulled himself free and swung up and onto the rafter beam. Will leaped up, too, and the fight continued. Back and forth across the beam they fought, each more determined than the other to conquer his opponent. Finally, they both jumped back to the floor, and as they did, Jack reached behind him into the ashes of the furnace. Grabbing a handful of soot, he turned and threw it right into Will Turner's face. Will stumbled back, temporarily blinded. Once he had cleared the ashes from his face, he looked up. Pointed directly between his eyes was Jack's pistol.

"You cheated," Will cried.

Smiling, Jack shrugged. He was a pirate. What did the young blacksmith expect? Jack began to once again move to the door. But Will blocked his path, undeterred by the weapon in his face. Cocking the gun, Jack took a threatening step forward. "You're lucky boy—this shot's not meant for you."

Will was about to ask who the shot was meant for, when he saw a hand holding an empty bottle rise up over Jack's head. Then, with a thud, it came down, shattering. Jack crumpled to the ground. Mr. Brown, the blacksmith, stood over Jack's body with a look of confusion on his face.

At that moment, the front and back doors of the shop flew open and the room filled with marines. Commodore Norrington strode forward and surveyed the shop. With a smile, he moved closer to Jack. "I believe you will always remember this as the day Captain Jack Sparrow *almost* escaped," he said with a laugh.

Norrington left the shop, followed by a group of marines dragging out one semiconscious, groaning, and thoroughly *captured* Jack Sparrow.

As night fell on Port Royal, the fog grew thicker, blanketing the streets, houses, and harbor in an eerie mist. People rushed home to the warmth of their hearths while in the taverns that lined the streets, men sat at wooden tables, warming themselves with ale and idle chat. Sitting high atop the cliff, Fort Charles was left untouched by the fog. It stood watch over the shrouded and still town.

But out on the water, something moved.

The shape of a ship grew clearer as it cut through the fog and entered the harbor. From its masts flew tattered black sails, and the ship itself seemed to be made of shadow. No sound came from its decks as it grew ever closer to the town. Suddenly, the fog thinned, and from the topmast, a single black flag could be seen flying. As it snapped back and forth in the wind, a skull and crossbones became visible . . . a sinister smile on its bony face. . . .

Meanwhile, sitting in a jail cell in Fort Charles, Captain Jack Sparrow leaned against the prison's rock wall, his hat pulled low over his eyes. The fog that had covered the town below was of no consequence to the pirate. At the moment, he was too distracted by the thought of his hanging in the morning and the hapless prisoners in the cell beside him.

The prisoners were crouched down and pressed against the bars of their cell, intent on one thing—escape. One of them held an old bone through the bars, waving it in front of a mangy dog that held a ring of keys in its mouth, while another held out a rope to the mutt. If they could get the dog over to the cell, they would have the keys, and a way out. Slowly, Jack lifted his head. "You can keep doing that forever," he said wisely. "That dog's never going to move."

"Excuse us if we ain't resigned ourselves to the gallows just yet," one of the men retorted.

Jack smiled, one corner of his mouth lifting to reveal his gold teeth. Then he lowered his head and once again slipped into silence. It looked like he and his fellow prisoners had but one fate—the gallows.

Back in the governor's mansion, Elizabeth Swann shivered in her bed. The eerie fog had crept into her chamber, making sleep impossible. Holding an unread book open in front of her, Elizabeth allowed Estrella to place a bed warmer at her feet.

"There you go, miss. It was a difficult day for you, I'm sure," the woman said gently, patting the sheets down and making sure the heat was not too much.

"I suspected Commodore Norrington would propose," Elizabeth said with a sigh. "But I was still not entirely prepared for it." Her thoughts drifted back to the moment at Fort Charles and Norrington's stammering request. Could he truly imagine they would make a good match? What of love? Surely the commodore could not be in love with her—they were very different types of people. "He's a fine man," Elizabeth continued. "The sort any woman *should* dream of marrying."

Estrella raised her eyebrows and leaned

closer, as if about to share an important secret. "That Will Turner . . . *he's* a fine man," she said softly.

From the bed, Elizabeth looked up sharply. Will Turner. Just the mention of his name sent color rushing to her cheeks. The way he had treated her earlier in the day, and for Estrella to imply . . . it was too much. With a sharp word, she sent the maid from the room and picked up her book. To be lost in words would be a lovely distraction. But she could not focus. The words on the page blurred. Absently her hand went to her neck, toying with the Medallion that still hung there.

Suddenly, the flame of the lamp beside her bed flickered and then lowered. Reaching over, Elizabeth tried to turn it back up. But it wouldn't work and the next moment, the light went out completely—pitching the room into darkness.

Inside the blacksmith's shop, Will Turner was hard at work, hammering out a piece of iron. With every hit, he tried to erase the events of the day. The morning at Governor Swann's, Elizabeth's fall, and then the run-in with that wily pirate. But it was no use. Pausing to catch his breath, Will walked over to one of the forge's windows and looked out. But he could not see far. Fog covered the streets, buildings, and signs. Will felt a shiver down his spine and had a strange feeling, like he was being watched. Reaching up, he pulled an ax off the wall and walked outside. As he looked up and down the alley, he almost expected someone to walk out of the shadows. But other than a lone cat that ran past, he was alone. . . .

Commodore Norrington and Governor Swann walked along the parapet that surrounded Fort Charles. On one side was the Caribbean, and on the other a courtyard, from which the shadow of the gallows could be made out. The two men were lost in thought as they paced, their hands behind their backs.

"Has my daughter given you an answer yet?" the governor asked, breaking the silence.

"No," Norrington answered. "She hasn't."

Suddenly, the stillness of the night was shattered by a loud boom, and the dark sky lit up. "Cannon fire!" Norrington shouted as the two men were sent flying. When the dust settled, they glanced at each other in panic. Who was attacking them? Who had arrived in Port Royal?

Inside the prison, the explosions rocked the cells. Leaping up, Jack rushed to the small barred window and looked out into the dark. A smile formed at the corners of his mouth as explosions lit up the night sky.

"I know those guns!" he shouted happily. "It's the *Pearl*."

Beside him, the prisoners' faces grew pale. The *Black Pearl*? They had heard the stories of the dreaded ship. For over ten years she had sailed the waters of the Caribbean, preying on towns and vessels. Without warning, she would appear out of the night and attack, leaving nothing but chaos and destruction in her path. Walking over to the bars that separated their cell from Jack, the prisoners looked closely at the pirate. Jack stood with his face eagerly pressed against the window bars, a gleam in his eye.

"I've heard she never leaves any survivors," one of the other prisoners stammered.

"No survivors?" Jack said with a smile as another explosion rocked the prison. "Then where do the stories come from, I wonder?"

The *Black Pearl* moved steadily closer, its cannons blasting. Down at the docks, sailors ran for cover as the ground beneath their feet exploded, sending wood and dirt flying into the sky. Within moments, the *Black Pearl* had all but destroyed the docks of Port Royal. Even the fog seemed to be blasted away under the pirate ship's assault. Men, women, and children ran screaming through the streets in search of safety.

With lightning speed, the crew of the *Black Pearl* dropped the longboats into the choppy water and rowed ashore. Carrying torches, swords, and guns, they swarmed the beach. Their clothes were torn and faded, and their faces were creased with dirt. Two of the pirates stopped for a moment and looked around. They made an odd pair—Ragetti was tall and skinny with a mop of dirty blond hair, while Pintel was short and squat, his head bald except at the sides where patches of long, straggly gray hair hung down. As they took in the chaotic scene, they both smiled, revealing two sets of very dirty teeth. Holding out a wooden eye, Ragetti spit on it and then rubbed it clean before placing it in his empty eye socket. Then, with a nod, they took off, following the rest of the *Black Pearl*'s crew into Port Royal.

Inside the blacksmith's forge, Will Turner listened as the sound of the attack got closer. Glass shattered as pirates threw explosives into random windows and gunshots rang out from every direction. Will quickly began to gather weapons. His fingers closed around an ax which he placed in his belt before grabbing a sword from the table. Fully armed, he ran outside.

A young woman ran past, chased by a maniacal pirate. Her sharp screams cut the deafening noise of the attack. Acting quickly, Will reached for his belt, pulled the ax out, and sent it sailing through the air—straight into the back of the pirate. The man fell where he was, his laugh silenced. Will retrieved his ax and ran off, the blade of his sword flashing.

Chapter 7

Elizabeth Swann stood on a balcony of the governor's mansion and stared at the terrible scene in front of her. Through the fog and smoke that filled the sky, she could make out the buildings in the town—or what was left of them. Fires raged all over the harbor and docks, illuminating the night with an unnatural glow. As Elizabeth watched, cannons continued to boom, and from Fort Charles, the sound of heavy gunfire could be heard.

Suddenly, the gate to the mansion was thrown open and pirates rushed into view. Elizabeth gasped. Turning, she ran inside and headed toward the top of the stairs. Reaching the landing that looked out over the foyer, she saw the butler approaching the front door.

"Don't," she started to shout. But it was too late. The butler opened the door to a mob of pirates, led by Pintel and Ragetti. Pintel aimed his gun directly at the butler.

"Hello chum," said Pintel, firing the gun.

As the butler crumpled to the ground, Elizabeth screamed. Pintel looked up and smiled, the gun still smoking in his hand. Glancing at Ragetti, the two dashed for the stairs in hot pursuit of Elizabeth.

Terrified, Elizabeth ran back up the stairs to her room, slamming the door and locking it. Estrella was right behind her, looking as terrified as Elizabeth felt.

"Miss Swann," she whispered. "They come to kidnap you?"

Elizabeth stared at Estrella in shock. The girl was right. She was the governor's daughter, after all, and would be very valuable in a trade if captured. The sound of a body slamming against the door snapped Elizabeth into action. As the door shook and the knob rattled, Elizabeth pushed Estrella back and out of sight. "They haven't seen you. Hide, and first chance, run for the fort," she ordered.

Suddenly, the door gave way and Pintel and Ragetti burst into the room just in time to see the flash of Elizabeth's white dress as she darted into the adjoining room. They raced after her.

Elizabeth, however, was not going to hide. She grabbed the closest thing to a weapon she had—the heavy pan filled with hot coals that served as a bed warmer. As Pintel entered the room, she swung, hitting him square in the face and knocking him to the ground. While he lay on the ground groaning, she swung again, this time aiming for Ragetti. But the tall pirate reached up, and with one hand, stopped Elizabeth in mid-swing. Laughing, he watched as she struggled to pull the pan away from him.

"Boo," he said with a laugh.

Glancing up at her raised hand, Elizabeth cocked an eyebrow. Ragetti followed her gaze, looking confused by the girl's lack of fear. Then, with one quick pull of her finger, she flipped the heated pan's latch and the lid flipped open, dropping ash and burning coals onto Ragetti's upturned face. Screaming, the pirate let go of Elizabeth.

Without a backward glance, Elizabeth ran out of the room and headed toward the foyer staircase. On the landing that overlooked the foyer, Elizabeth's eyes grew wide. All around her pirates raced back and forth. Some were chasing the governor's servants, while others dragged loot away. Elizabeth flew down the stairs, her white bedroom slippers a blur beneath her dressing gown. Pintel and Ragetti followed close behind.

Just as she reached the bottom of the stairs, Ragetti leaped over the balcony and landed in front of Elizabeth, a flaming torch in his hand. He let out a vicious growl, forcing Elizabeth to take a step back—closer to Pintel. Frantically, Elizabeth looked back and forth between the two pirates, unsure of what to do. She was trapped. Suddenly, a low whine filled the air, causing Elizabeth and the two men to glance curiously toward the mansion's front door. Moments later, the wall exploded as a cannonball ripped through the room, taking down a pirate as he struggled with an armful of gold and jewels.

With Pintel and Ragetti distracted, Elizabeth once again took off at a run, ducking into the dining room. Quickly, she placed a candelabrum over the doorknobs, temporarily locking out the pirates. As the pirates cursed and pulled at the door, Elizabeth frantically searched the room for a weapon. Her eyes landed on a pair of crossed swords hanging on a piece of carved wood above the fireplace. She reached up to grab one, but it was stuck in the wood. The swords were nothing more than decoration. The rattling at the door grew louder. Diving into the small linen closet, Elizabeth shut the door behind her and waited as quietly as she could.

Just as Elizabeth shut the closet door behind her, Pintel and Ragetti broke through the door to the room. But the room looked empty to the pirates. Elizabeth was nowhere to be seen. In the dim torchlight, they noticed that one of the windows was open, its curtain blowing in the gentle night breeze.

"We know you're here, poppet," Pintel said in a singsong tone. "Come out, and we promise we won't hurt you."

Inside the closet, Elizabeth whimpered.

Pintel continued to pace around the room, his eyes scanning the walls. "We will find you, poppet . . . you've got something of ours, and it calls to us," he said. Then, with a smile, he added, "The gold calls to us."

Shrinking back against the linen-lined shelves of the closet, Elizabeth reached for her neck. The Medallion! Pulling it away from her neck, she held it in her fingertips, watching as a ray of light from outside caused it to spark and glow brighter. Suddenly, the light faded and the Medallion returned to darkness. Looking up, Elizabeth gasped. Staring back at her through a crack in the door, mere inches from her face, was Pintel.

"Hello, poppet," he said. He flung the closet door open. Cocking his gun, Pintel took one step forward. But Elizabeth's next words stopped him cold.

"Parley," she said. "I invoke the right of parley! According to the Code of the Brethren, set down by the pirates Morgan and Bartholomew, you must take me to your captain!"

Pintel glared at Elizabeth. "I know the Code," he said slowly, his eyes flashing in anger. The girl was smart. To invoke parley guaranteed that she would remain safe—for a little while longer. As Ragetti took a threatening step forward, his knife drawn, Pintel put out a hand to stop him. "She wants to be taken to the captain," he said, "and we must honor the Code."

Chapter 8

While Elizabeth was busy invoking the right of parley, Will Turner found himself in the middle of a sword fight with a very large, very bald, and very angry pirate. Suddenly, Will felt a chain wrap around his wrist and he was dragged up against his large adversary. Looking up into the bald man's eyes, Will grimaced. This was the end for sure. Closing his eyes, he waited for the death blow, but it never came. Instead, a bomb whizzed out of the melee, landing a direct hit on a nearby building. Fortunately for Will, the explosion also happened to unhook a hanging sign, which slammed the bald pirate square in the chest.

Freed from the pirate's grasp, Will turned and headed back into the streets of Port Royal. He had only managed to take a few steps, when a flash of white caught his attention. Looking over, he saw Elizabeth being dragged toward the harbor by two vile-looking pirates. Feeling his gaze on her, she turned, her eyes seeking him out across the street.

"Elizabeth," he said to himself.

Just then, another group of pirates passed. Reaching out, one of them brought a heavy candleholder down on Will's head. With a groan, Will collapsed to the ground.

Meanwhile, in his prison cell, Jack Sparrow stared out his window, watching as bombs continued to blow Port Royal to bits. The four men jailed next to Jack had long since given up their attempts to lure the dog with the keys closer, and now sat defeated. Glancing up into the sky, Jack saw the faint outline of the moon, barely visible behind the thick clouds of smoke.

Suddenly, a bomb burst clear through the prison wall into the cell next to Jack's, ripping a giant hole in the stone. Hazy moonlight poured into the now-open cell, illuminating the four prisoners as they leaped to their feet and headed for the hole. One of the convicts turned back to Jack.

"My sympathies, friend," he said. "You've

no manner of luck at all!" Then, along with the others, he slipped outside to freedom.

No luck at all? Jack was not so sure. Left alone, he walked over to examine what was left of his former neighbors' prison wall. The unfortunate nature of events had left both the bars of his own cell and the outside wall intact. The other prisoner had been right. He had no luck—there was no way for him to get out. Sighing, he walked over to the front of the cell just as the clouds parted, revealing a bright and full moon.

Reaching through the bars, his rings gleaming in the moonlight, Jack picked up the bone the other prisoners had dropped and began to wave it. "Come here, doggie," he called. "It's just you and me now. You and old Jack." From under a bench down the hall, the guard dog lifted his head. Slowly, he crawled out and began to make his way toward Jack, his tail wagging back and forth timidly. "That's it," Jack said, attempting to sound sincere. But he was a pirate, and the dog was not moving fast enough. He couldn't help but add, "You filthy, mangy, stinking cur." The dog let out one whimper, and then Jack watched in horror as it took off down the hall—with the keys.

Just then, a shout came from the top of the entranceway that led to the prison. With a mighty crash, a red-coated marine came flying down the stairs, and smashing into the stone wall, was knocked unconscious. Close behind the marine came two pirates—known to their crew as Koehler and Twigg. Both were tall and wore the grungy garb of men long at sea. Koehler had a head full of long, black dreadlocks, and Twigg wore a tight hat. As they drew closer to Jack's cell, he stood up and casually placed his hands through the bars of his cell.

"Well, well, well," said Koehler as he sheathed his sword. "Look what we have here, Twigg. It's Captain Jack Sparrow." He leaned forward and spit at Jack's feet.

His arms still through the cell bars, Jack looked first at Koehler and then down at his feet, a puzzled expression on his face. But he remained silent.

"Last time I saw you," said Twigg, "you were all alone on a godforsaken island, shrinking into the distance." Laughing, he turned to Koehler and added, "His fortunes haven't improved much."

Jack put his face right up against the bars.

"Worry about your own fortunes, gentlemen," he said with a smug smile. "The deepest circle of Davy Jones's locker is reserved for betrayers . . . and mutineers."

With a growl, Koehler reached through the bars of the cell. His fingers wrapping tightly around Jack's throat, forcing him to lean back—right into a shaft of moonlight. As Jack clutched the pirate's arm trying to free himself, his eyes widened. In the moonlight, Koehler's arm appeared to be nothing but the bones of a skeleton.

"So there *is* a curse," he said. "That is interesting."

Koehler's fingers tightened. "You know nothing of pain," he said with a snarl. Then, with one final squeeze, he released Jack.

As the pair walked off, Jack stepped back up to the bars. "That's *very* interesting," he said softly. And as the pirates' footsteps faded away, Jack smiled. The night had just taken a decidedly positive turn.

For Elizabeth Swann, however, the night had taken a decidedly *negative* turn. She now found herself sitting at the prow of a longboat, being rowed toward the hull of a massive, black ship. Looking up, her gaze fell upon the bow of the ship, from which hung the ornately carved figure of a woman. In her outstretched hands, she held a bird. Elizabeth, shivering and afraid, couldn't help but see the irony in having such a peaceful figure for such a horrid ship. As the moon slipped behind thick clouds, the figurehead disappeared into the darkness.

From the ship's sides, cannons continued to fire, blasting more holes in Port Royal and filling the air around the ship with ash and powder. Elizabeth's eyes scanned her surroundings, taking in the tall masts from which heavy black sails hung. A few lights illuminated the deck, casting a pale glow over the rough wood and creating eerie shadows. And from onboard, she could hear the shouts of the pirates and the sound of metal, presumably loot, being thrown around.

All too soon, the longboat pulled up beside the ship and Pintel and Ragetti pushed Elizabeth unceremoniously onto the deck. As she stumbled on her long, white nightgown, her eyes caught sight of a man standing in the shadows—removed from the chaos onboard. But it was only a glimpse. Looking around, her heart began to pound faster and she struggled to breathe. There were pirates everywhere. She heard men shouting in different languages as bodies pushed by her, unbothered by her presence. But there was one member of the crew who was indeed bothered by Elizabeth. The Bo'sun, a tall, dark man with tattooed dots surrounding his eyes and mouth, approached.

"I didn't know we was taking captives," he said in a heavily accented voice.

Keeping a firm hold on Elizabeth's arm, Pintel explained. "She's invoked the right of parley," he said, "with Captain Barbossa."

Pulling free, Elizabeth strode forward. "I am here to . . ." she began. But she was silenced when the Bo'sun reached over and slapped her across the face—hard. Shocked, Elizabeth stepped back, a hand on her stinging cheek.

The Bo'sun raised his hand to strike again when another hand reached out and grabbed his wrist. "You'll not lay a hand on those under the protection of parley," said Captain Barbossa, his voice gravelly with age, but still powerful.

Elizabeth looked over at Barbossa, curious to see what type of man could captain such a crew. At first sight, he seemed more gentleman than pirate. Though his bearded face was lined and weathered, and the whites of his eyes were more yellow than white, he wore a fine feathered hat and long, black dress coat. A monkey wearing a white dress shirt perched on his shoulder.

"My apologies, miss," Barbossa said.

"Captain Barbossa," Elizabeth began boldly. "I am here to negotiate the cessation of hostilities against Port Royal."

Around her, several of the crew chuckled, while a smile played at the corner of Barbossa's mouth. Shaking his head and looking around, the captain answered. "There was a lot of long words in there, miss, and we're not but humble pirates," he said, laughing. "What is it that you want?"

Elizabeth paused. "I want you to leave and never come back," she replied proudly.

Now all of the crew laughed. A silly girl in a nightdress was asking their captain to just up and sail away. It was indeed a laughable request. And Barbossa seemed to agree. "I am disinclined to acquiesce to your request," he said, throwing Elizabeth's fancy words back in her face. Then, with a smile, he added, "Means no."

"Very well," Elizabeth replied, raising her chin proudly. Then she remembered something Pintel and Ragetti had said. They were looking for something she had. Something that was theirs. In one swift move she reached up and ripped the Medallion from her neck. Storming over to the ship's rail, she threw her arm over the water, letting the Medallion dangle from her fingertips. "I'll drop it," she said threateningly.

In the light from the cannon fire, the Medallion lit up. For a moment, the captain's eyes grew wide and he shifted uneasily. Regaining his composure, he gestured around the ship. "My holds are bursting with swag," he pointed out. "That bit of shine matters to us? Why?"

Elizabeth felt herself grow even madder. Glaring at Barbossa, she shouted, "Because it's what you're searching for." Then she added, "I recognize this ship. I saw it eight years ago, when we made the crossing from England."

"Did you, now?" Barbossa replied.

Elizabeth's eyes jumped from Barbossa to his crew, looking for a sign that the captain was bluffing. All eyes were on her and the dangling Medallion. "Fine," she said. "I suppose if it *is* worthless, there's no sense in me keeping it. . . ." As her voice trailed off, she opened her fingers, allowing the Medallion's gold chain to slip through her fingers toward the water below.

Barbossa and his men leaped forward, shouting "No!" Her hand still grasping the chain, Elizabeth smiled and nodded. So she had been right. The Medallion was what the pirates were looking for, after all.

With a throaty chuckle, Barbossa moved closer, and Elizabeth's smile began to fade. While she held the Medallion, she had some element of control over the situation. She dared not lose it.

Pulling the gold closer to her, she steeled herself against the pirate.

"You have a name, missy?" he asked, giving her a long, hard look.

"Elizabeth," she began, before stopping herself. If she revealed her last name, Barbossa would surely figure out that she was the governor's daughter. She could not risk it. Looking down at the Medallion, she had an idea. "Turner," she finished quickly. "I'm a maid in the governor's household."

Barbossa's eyes grew wide and he turned to face his men. "Miss *Turner*," he announced. At the mention of the name Turner, the men began to mumble, while Pintel uttered a single name. "Bootstrap."

"Very well," Barbossa said, once again focusing his attention on Elizabeth. "You hand that over, we'll put your town to our rudder and ne'er return." Holding out his hand, he waited as Elizabeth considered the exchange. Reluctantly, she dropped the Medallion into his open palm. Barbossa's monkey, who up until that point had simply sat on the captain's shoulder looking bored, leaped down and grabbed the Medallion.

Then, with a screech, it jumped onto a mast line and into the rigging. Elizabeth's bargaining chip was gone.

Without another word, Barbossa turned and started back toward the rear of the ship. Calling out orders to the crew, the Bo'sun prepared to leave Port Royal. But no one made a move to send Elizabeth back. "Wait!" she shouted, chasing after Barbossa. "You must return me to shore! According to the Code. . . "

Barbossa whipped around, cutting her off. "First, your return to shore was not part of our negotiations, nor our agreement and so I 'must' do nothing. And secondly, you must be a pirate for the Pirate's Code to apply. And you're not." He paused, a smile creasing his weather-beaten face. "And thirdly . . . the Code is more what you'd call *guidelines* than actual rules."

Elizabeth felt hands grab her arms as Pintel and Ragetti began to drag her away. But not before Barbossa got in his final word. "Welcome aboard the *Black Pearl* . . . Miss Turner."

In Port Royal, Will Turner awoke with a headache. Reaching up, he winced as his fingers brushed the spot where he had been hit the night before. Blinking his dark brown eyes, he looked around. The smoke and fog that had covered the town only a few hours earlier were gone, replaced by blue skies and sun. But all around, signs of the pirate attack could be seen. Rising to his feet, Will looked out at the harbor. It was a disaster. Ships lay burning at anchor, and the docks were nothing more than splintered wood.

Suddenly, the image of Elizabeth being dragged by pirates toward the harbor returned to his mind. Without thinking, he took off at a run.

Moments later, he burst into the courtyard of Fort Charles. Men in red uniforms carried the wounded, while others attempted to clear away debris. But Will did not notice. His eyes landed on the man standing in a stone archway, his gaze riveted to a map in front of him. It was Commodore Norrington. Despite the night's events, the commodore looked remarkably well put together. His blue uniform was crisp and his white wig was pulled tightly and neatly against his scalp. On either side of him, armed marines stood watch, their sabers pointed high.

"They've taken her!" Will shouted, rushing up the steps and coming to a stop in front of the commodore. "They've taken Elizabeth."

"Mr. Murtogg," Norrington replied, not even looking up from the map, "remove this man."

Will stared at the commodore in disbelief. He was not going to look for Elizabeth? It was beyond belief. "We have to save her!" Will exclaimed.

From behind the commodore, a figure turned and moved closer to Will. It was the governor. Where Norrington appeared calm and in control, the governor was clearly shaken. "And where do you propose we start?" he asked Will. "If you have any information that concerns my daughter, then please—share it. If anyone does, tell me!"

"That Jack Sparrow," Murtogg stammered. "He talked about the *Black Pearl*. . . ."

Will leaned forward eagerly. Jack Sparrow! The pirate! Of course he would know of the *Pearl*. "Ask him where it is!" he said aloud to Norrington.

"The pirates who invaded this fort left Sparrow locked up in his cell," Norrington retorted. "Ergo, they are not his allies."

A loud thud shook the table on which the map rested. Will's ax was now buried deep in the wood.

But Norrington had dealt with worse things than an angered blacksmith. Reaching over, he pulled the ax out of the wood and palmed it in his hand. "Mr. Turner," he said, making his way around the table. "You have nothing of value to contribute here." Then, pausing, he reached out and grabbed Will's arm. In a whisper, he added, "Do not make the mistake of thinking you are the only man here who cares for Elizabeth." Without another word, he pushed him out of the archway.

The discussion with Norrington was over. But Will had one more person to visit. He headed toward the prison . . . and Jack Sparrow.

Inside his cell, Captain Jack Sparrow was unaware of the kidnapping of Elizabeth Swann or of Will Turner's plan to get her back. Sunlight filtered through the cell as Jack tried in vain to pick the lock of his cell—with a bone. Suddenly, the door to the prison creaked open. Leaving the bone in the lock, he fell to the straw-covered ground and lay there, one arm behind his head in order to look inconspicuous.

It was Will Turner. He was still fuming over his run-in with Norrington. Noticing that only one cell in the prison had remained intact from the night before, he stormed over to it and saw the reclining pirate.

"You. Sparrow," Will said. "You familiar with that ship? The *Black Pearl*?"

"I've heard of it," Jack drawled, not bothering to lift his head from the floor. He recognized the lad from the blacksmith shop. It was he who had helped get him captured and placed in this horrid prison in the first place.

"Where does it make berth?" Will asked.

"Where does it make berth?" Jack repeated, once again raising his head and looking at Will in disbelief. He lowered his head back to the ground and began to wave one hand in the air absently.

"Have you not heard the stories? Captain Barbossa and his crew of miscreants sail from the dreaded *Isla de Muerta* . . . an island that cannot be found." He paused and looked up at Will, "Except by those who already know where it is."

Will gazed down at the pirate, struggling to control his temper. "The ship's real enough," he said through clenched teeth. "Where is it?"

"Why ask me?"

"They took Miss Swann," Will replied, tightly gripping the bars of the cell.

At the mention of "miss," Jack raised himself up onto his elbows, his interest piqued. "Ah, so it is that you found a girl," he said with a knowing smile. "Well, if you're intending to brave all, hasten to her rescue, and so win fair lady's heart, you'll have to do it alone, mate. I see no profit in it for me."

"I can get you out of here," Will answered. Quickly he pointed out that he had helped build the cells and knew how to break in. Grabbing a nearby bench, he jimmied it into the bars and paused, looking down at the pirate. He would do no more until Sparrow agreed to help him.

Still lying on the ground, Jack cocked his head and looked at Will suspiciously. "What is your name, boy?" he asked.

"Will Turner."

Upon hearing the name, Jack sat up. "Short for William, I imagine. No doubt named for your father?" Jumping to his feet, he walked over and smiled through the bars at Will. "I've changed my mind. You spring me from this cell, and I'll take you to the *Black Pearl* and your bonnie lass."

"Agreed," Will said.

Putting all his weight on the bench that was still wedged in the cell door, Will pushed. With a creak and groan, the door sprang off its hinges. Grabbing his hat, pistol, belt, and Compass, Jack headed out of the prison. He was free!

The next morning, Will found himself underneath a bridge looking out at Port Royal's harbor. In front of him stood Jack Sparrow, his hat safely back on his head. Men in uniform were frantically running up and down the loading docks, filling the hold of a smaller ship docked nearby. Behind it, the HMS *Dauntless* loomed, a British flag flying from its stern. "We're going to steal that ship?" Will asked, gazing out to the *Dauntless*.

"Commandeer," Jack corrected. "We're going to commandeer *that* ship." He pointed out toward the closer, and much smaller, ship that was being loaded.

Gesturing for Will to follow, Jack tiptoed to an overturned rowboat. He had a plan. But first, he had to get them to the *Dauntless*. Lifting up the rowboat, the pair quickly ducked underneath it and walked down to the water's edge, pulling the boat under the waves before anyone spotted them. Safely in the water, breathing the air trapped beneath the overturned rowboat, Will looked over at Jack. "This is either madness or brilliance," he said.

"Remarkable how often those two traits coincide," Jack replied.

Moments later, they sneaked aboard the *Dauntless* and moved toward the small crew that manned the decks. "Everybody stay calm!" Jack shouted, holding his pistol steady. "We're taking over the ship!"

The marines burst into laughter. "This ship cannot be crewed by two men. You'll never make it out of the bay," one of them said, chuckling.

Jack rolled his head back and smiled. He was Captain Jack Sparrow! He never resisted a challenge.

Moments later, from the dock beside the *Interceptor,* a shout rose up. Out on the water, rowing *away* from the *Dauntless* was the ship's crew. Reaching into his belt, Commodore Norrington pulled out a spyglass and lifted it to his eye. Beyond the longboat, the sails of the *Dauntless* were being lowered. Norrington could make out Sparrow on deck, his arms flailing in the air as he ordered Will Turner about. "That is, without doubt, the worst pirate I have ever seen," Norrington commented.

Back aboard the *Dauntless,* Jack turned and glanced over his shoulder. His plan was working! Norrington was dropping the sails on the *Interceptor* and preparing for pursuit. While the *Dauntless* was heavily armed, she was not swift.

The *Interceptor* quickly drew alongside the bigger ship and dropped a gangplank across the rail. Quickly the men boarded the *Dauntless,* prepared to capture the two thieves. But no one was aboard.

Too late, Norrington heard the sound of a splash and looked back just in time to see the *Interceptor* pulling away. Jack was at the wheel of the smaller boat. He tipped his hat to Norrington.

"Thank you, Commodore," he shouted, "for getting us ready to make way! We'd've had a hard time of it ourselves."

From his spot beside the commodore, a marine watched in admiration as the ship faded into the distance, fast becoming nothing more than a speck on the horizon. "That's got to be the best pirate I've ever seen," he said.

Chapter 12

Out at sea, the *Interceptor* cut through the water, her sails taut in the breeze. Standing at the rail, Captain Jack Sparrow checked the lines, while at a nearby barrel, Will Turner methodically sharpened the blade of his sword. High atop the main mast, the *Interceptor*'s flag waved in the wind, and waves crashed against the bow of the ship as she made her way steadily onward under the bright blue sky. For a moment there was silence, as the two men busied themselves with their tasks. Both had much on their minds.

"When I was a lad in England," Will said, not looking up from his sword, "my mother raised me herself. After she died, I came out here . . . looking for my father." Pausing from his sword sharpening, he looked over at Jack, waiting for the captain's response.

Testing a line, Jack looked up into the

rigging and then headed for the ship's wheel. "Is that so?" he asked innocently as he passed by Will.

But Will suspected that the pirate knew more than he let on. Cocking his head, he watched the pirate continue to crew the ship—by himself. Will's brow furrowed. Jumping up, he approached Jack. "My father. Bill Turner?" he pressed. "At the jail—it was only *after* you learned my name that you agreed to help. I'm not a simpleton, Jack. You knew my father."

Jack did not bother to look at Will as he spoke, his attention apparently focused on keeping the ship sailing. But the captain heard every word. If he were to sail this ship, he would need the boy—and he would need him to stop being so chatty. Sighing, he stood up and turned toward Will, his tan and weathered face mere inches from the blacksmith's. "I knew him," he said. "Probably one of the few who knew him as William Turner. Most everyone just called him Bootstrap or Bootstrap Bill." Moving away from Will, Jack took his place at the wheel before adding, "Good man. Good pirate. I swear, you look just like him."

At the word "pirate," Will's head jerked up

and pain flashed across his face. His father? A pirate? All these years, he had dreamed of his father, thought of him as a merchant marine and a law-abiding civilian. If Jack was telling the truth, everything he had come to believe was a lie and his father was just another one of the group he hated most in the world—pirates. Before he could stop himself, he drew his sword.

Hearing the swish of metal, Jack sighed. "Put it away, son," he said calmly, his hands never leaving the wheel of the ship. Realizing that Will was not going to let up, Jack did what any self-respecting pirate would do—he cheated. With a mighty shove, he spun the wheel, causing the ship's heavy boom to whip over the deck. Will, unused to life on the sea, was caught unaware. A second later, he found himself dangling off the boom and over the water.

Having Will's complete and utter attention, Jack decided to clarify a few matters before they sailed any farther. Picking up Will's sword, he pointed it straight at him. "The only rules that really matter are these: what a man can do. And what a man can't do." Pausing, he moved back toward the wheel. "You can accept that your father was a pirate and a good man . . . or you can't. But, pirate's in your blood, boy, so you're going to have to square with that someday."

Still hanging dangerously over the sea, Will kicked his legs and struggled to keep hold of the boom. Jack's words were painful to hear, but the pirate had a point—a twisted one, but a point nevertheless. With another push of the wheel, Jack swung the boom back over the deck, and Will fell to the ground, his arms shaking.

Will assessed his situation. Jack had not killed him—and he had promised to help him rescue Elizabeth. Reluctantly, Will agreed to follow Jack, and pleased with Will's decision, Jack set the course. He needed a crew for his new ship and there was only one place he knew that would satisfy this need—the rough and tumble pirate town of Tortuga.

Ah, Tortuga. Walking through one of the many alleys that littered the port, Jack smiled. To be a pirate meant to love Tortuga, with its crowded taverns, feisty women, and flowing ale.

Will Turner, on the other hand, was not yet convinced of Tortuga's charms. The town was dirty and smelly, and the streets echoed with the sound of fighting and gunfire. Everywhere he looked, men and women caroused about, shouting and laughing. Looking up, Will watched as a man leaned back and began to pour rum from two different mugs down his throat, spilling the amber liquid all over himself. Nearby, three heavy women, their ample chests spilling out above tight corsets, laughed loudly.

Seeing Will's dismay, Jack piped up. "I tell you, Will," he said, "if every town in the world was like this one, no man would ever feel unwanted." Just as he finished speaking, a woman in a bright red dress with equally red hair stalked over to them. "Scarlett!" Jack said, his shiny grin growing wider as he took in the woman's familiar figure. But Scarlett was not nearly as happy to see Jack. Bringing her hand back, she slapped him hard across the cheek and then stalked off.

A few minutes later, Will found himself standing behind one of Tortuga's many taverns—the Faithful Bride. In front of him, an old sailor lay in the mud, his head resting on the belly of a sleeping pig. It was Joshamee Gibbs—the very same seaman who had warned Elizabeth of pirates eight long years before. Time had not treated him well—his beard was now more gray than black, his clothes were tattered, and he smelled of pig and ale. But that didn't appear to bother Jack. Gibbs was a mate. Grabbing a nearby water pail, Jack doused the man, causing him to sit up, his gun drawn.

"Ah, Jack," he said, when he shook the water from his eyes. "You know it's bad luck to wake a man when he's sleeping."

"Well, fortunately," Jack told his friend, "I know how to counter it. The man who did the waking buys the man who was sleeping a drink." Leaning down, he pulled Gibbs to his feet and together the three men made their way into the tavern.

Moments later, Gibbs and Jack sat at a table, tankards of ale in front of them. Will stood a little ways off, eyeing the debauchery around him. Glancing around to make sure no one was listening, Jack lowered his voice and leaned close to Gibbs. "I'm going after the *Black Pearl*. I know where it's going to be, and I'm going to take it." Pausing, he added, "I need a crew."

"Jack, it's a fool's errand," sputtered Gibbs.

"What makes you think Barbossa will give up his ship to you?"

In the light from the candles that illuminated the tavern, Jack's eyes gleamed. "Let's just say, it's a matter of leverage." Tilting his head, he nodded in the direction of Will, who still stood watch, apparently unaware of what Jack was saying. Gibbs stared blankly at Jack. Again, the pirate nodded at Will.

"The kid?" Gibbs asked, confused.

Jack nodded. "That is the child of Bootstrap Bill Turner." Then, pausing for dramatic effect, he added, "His *only* child."

Gibbs looked once again at Will. The young blacksmith seemed out of place among the rough-and-tumble tavern crowd. But Gibbs just smiled. Bootstrap Bill's only child. This was indeed fortuitous. Looking back at Jack, his grin grew wider. "Leverage, says you," he said wisely. "I feel a change in the wind, says I. I'll find us a crew."

Leaning back in his chair, Captain Jack Sparrow smiled. He was one step closer to Barbossa . . . and the *Pearl*.

Far from the port of Tortuga, the *Black Pearl* sailed under a moonlit sky. As she cut through the dark waves, her sails appeared to be nothing more than shadow, and the only light on deck came from the moon, which was filtered by the clouds. High above the stern, candlelit windows stretched across the boat's length, casting an eerie glow on the water below.

Locked inside the cabin, Elizabeth Swann stood in her dressing gown and wrap, staring absently at the flickering candles that filled the room. Only her eyes gave away her discomfort and fatigue. Suddenly, the cabin door burst open and the two pirates who had viciously dragged her away from her home—Pintel and Ragetti—entered. Pintel carried a deep red silk gown.

"You'll be dining with the captain," Pintel informed Elizabeth. Then, nodding to the gown in his arms, he added, "And he requests you wear this."

Sticking out her chin and giving the men her stormiest glare, Elizabeth retorted, "You can tell the captain that I am disinclined to acquiesce to his request."

But the pair just laughed, revealing their dirty and rotten teeth. Miss Swann had no choice. It was dining with the captain in his cabin—or with the crew. Huffing, Elizabeth reached out and grabbed the dress from Pintel. While the captain was horrid, dinner with the crew seemed even less appealing.

A short while later, Elizabeth sat at a table filled with food. The aroma of freshly cooked meat wafted through the cabin, causing her stomach to growl. Succulent goat, fresh seafood, hot bread, and juicy pieces of fruit covered every inch of the large table. At the head of the table, Captain Barbossa watched as Elizabeth picked up a piece of chicken and took a small bite. Her hand shook as she brought the meat to her lips. She was famished, but pirate ship or not, she would remain a lady.

Barbossa seemed to disagree. "No need to

stand on ceremony," he said, not touching his own plate. "You must be hungry."

He was right. Dropping her fork, Elizabeth picked up the chicken and tore into it, grease and sauce covering her lips and cheeks. As she ate, Barbossa watched, his hungry eyes never leaving Elizabeth's mouth. But still, he did not eat. Pouring a glass of wine, he offered it to his guest and watched once more as she gulped it down. Unaware of the captain's intense stare, Elizabeth continued to devour the food.

"And the apples," Barbossa said, holding out a green apple toward her. "One of those next."

Looking up, Elizabeth paused midbite, suddenly wary of Barbossa's offer. There was something peculiar in the way he was looking at her. Even his monkey was staring at her. Suddenly, a thought crossed Elizabeth's mind.

"It's poisoned," she said aloud, her face growing pale.

Barbossa laughed. "There would be no sense in killing you, Miss Turner." Reaching into his jacket, he pulled out Elizabeth's Medallion. "You don't know what this is, do you?" he asked, dangling it in front of her.

"A pirate medallion," Elizabeth answered, shrugging her shoulders.

"This is Aztec Gold," Barbossa went on, his voice growing deeper and more grave. "One of eight hundred and eighty-two identical pieces they delivered to Cortés himself. Blood money. But the greed of Cortés was insatiable . . . and so, the heathen gods placed upon the gold a terrible curse." He leaned in close to Elizabeth before adding, "Any mortal that removes but a piece from that chest shall be punished for all eternity."

Elizabeth raised her eyebrows. In Barbossa's hand, the Medallion flickered as the light played off its skull. But despite the captain's ominous words, Elizabeth was not afraid. "I hardly believe in ghost stories anymore, Captain Barbossa," she replied haughtily.

Barbossa chuckled knowingly. That was what he had thought when he first learned of the curse, he told Elizabeth. But ah, how quickly he had been proved wrong. He and his men found the chest on *Isla de Muerta* and plundered the gold, quickly spending it on food and drink. But slowly, something began to happen. Food no longer filled their bellies and drink did not quench their thirst. "We are cursed men, Miss Turner," he said, his voice a whisper in her ear. "Compelled by greed we were, but now we are consumed by it." Suddenly, as if the tale were too much for the monkey to bear, it began to shriek, drawing Barbossa's attention away from Elizabeth. While he was distracted, she slowly reached up and pulled a steak knife off the table and slipped it into the sleeve of her gown.

Unaware of Elizabeth's movements, Barbossa continued, "There is one way to end our curse. All the scattered pieces of gold must be restored, and the blood repaid." Pausing, Barbossa placed the monkey on his shoulder and handed to it Elizabeth's piece of gold. "Thanks to ye," he said, once again drawing close to her, "we have the final piece."

Still seated in her chair, Elizabeth shivered. "And the blood to be repaid?" she asked. "What of it?"

"That's why there's no sense to be killing you," Barbossa replied calmly. "Yet."

Elizabeth's eyes widened as realization dawned. It was her blood that would end the curse! Jumping up, she pulled the knife out of her sleeve and slashed at Barbossa, who quickly side-stepped out of the way. Racing around the table, she looked to the cabin door. If she could only get outside. But Barbossa was there, blocking her way. With a scream, she brought the knife down—stabbing him in the chest.

Gasping, she pulled away, expecting Barbossa to fall to the ground. But he didn't. "I'm curious," he said instead. "After killing me, what is it you planned to do next?"

Turning in terror, Elizabeth burst through the door of the cabin onto the main deck—and screamed. There, in front of her, where human sailors *should* have been, a crew of skeletons was at work swabbing the decks and coiling the lines. In the light of the moon, their bones glowed a bluish-white, and they were draped in tattered pieces of clothing. Screeching, Elizabeth tried to turn and run, but she fell, landing on a blanket in the cargo hold. A moment later, she was flung high into the air as skeletons pulled the blanket from beneath her. She came down, only to be caught by another skeleton as he swung by on a mast line. Terrified, she screamed again as she fell to the deck. All the while, the skeletons kept working on the ship, seemingly unbothered by her antics.

Desperate to get away from the crew, Elizabeth ran over and hid under a stairway. Gasping for breath, she let out another scream when the monkey swung down, landing in front of her face. It was a skeleton, too!

Once more, she jumped up, this time heading for the safety of the captain's cabin. But Barbossa was waiting for her in the shadows and he grabbed her, pulling her close. "Look!" he shouted. "The moonlight shows us for what we really are! We cannot die!" Laughing, he pushed Elizabeth out into the moonlight. As he stepped forward, the light hit his arm, and Elizabeth watched in disbelief as his flesh was replaced by bone.

"You best start believing in ghost stories," he said, finally stepping fully into the moonlight, turning his face into a grinning skull. "You're in one."

While Elizabeth Swann was busy facing a crew of cursed pirates, back in Tortuga Mr. Gibbs had managed to gather a ragtag group of sailors to crew the *Interceptor*. They now stood on the docks, awaiting Captain Sparrow's approval. Jack walked down the line, stopping periodically to question the men. Behind him followed Will, an unimpressed look on his face.

Indeed, it was not the most stellar crew. One of the men, known to the others as Cotton, had lost his tongue and couldn't speak. Instead, a brightly colored parrot who sat on his shoulder did all the talking for him. The other men looked weak and hungry, eager to take on work for the chance of a berth and a meal. However, there was one sailor who seemed saucier than the rest. His head tipped forward, a wide hat hiding his face, he shouted out a question to the captain, "What is the benefit for us?"

Walking over, Jack leaned down and lifted the brim of the sailor's hat. Just as he suspected—the he was really a she! More specifically, the she was Anamaria—the owner of one, now fully sunk, fishing dory named the *Jolly Mon.* In the bright Caribbean sun, her dark honey-colored skin glowed. But it was her eyes that were the most striking—the dark brown orbs looked at Jack with a mixture of anger and frustration. Reaching out, Anamaria slapped him across the face, causing Will to smirk. Slapping seemed to be a recurring theme. But Jack deserved it. After all, he had "borrowed" her boat without permission.

Unfortunately for Jack, Anamaria was a good sailor, and he needed her onboard. So, using his keen negotiation skills—and some help from Will, who promised Anamaria the *Interceptor*—he finally managed to convince her to join the crew. With a full crew, a stocked boat, and his trusty Compass, they were now ready. It was time to sail for *Isla de Muerta* . . . and the *Black Pearl.*

Later that night, as storms rocked the *Interceptor,* Will Turner struggled to keep his footing. The ship pitched and dipped as waves buffeted her sides, while above, the sails flapped angrily in the wind. Standing at the wheel, Jack stared down at his Compass, oblivious to the rain that soaked his jacket and poured off the corners of his hat. Despite the poor conditions, the captain seemed sure of himself and his heading.

"How can we find an island no one can find—with a compass that doesn't work?" Will asked Gibbs, who was helping him cleat a rather large and very wet line.

"The Compass doesn't point north," Gibbs agreed. "But we're not trying to find north, are we?" he added cryptically.

Leaving Will to figure out the riddle, Gibbs headed toward Jack. The slippery deck and pounding rain made it slow going, and by the time he reached the captain's side, Gibbs was in a foul mood. Jack, on the other hand, looked oddly happy.

"What's in your head as puts you in such a fine mood?" Gibbs asked.

Jack looked over at his mate. Then, with a knowing grin, he answered, "We're catching up!"

While the *Interceptor* was drawing closer to *Isla de Muerta*, the *Black Pearl* had already arrived. She lay

Captain Jack Sparrow—the notorious pirate—sails into Port Royal.

Elizabeth Swann discovers Will Turner's secret—he's a pirate!

Eight years after arriving in Port Royal, Governor Swann makes Captain Norrington a commodore.

Elizabeth finds life as the governor's daughter tiresome—she longs for adventure.

Jack pulls Elizabeth to safety, but it's not enough—he's still arrested for being a pirate.

Jack needs to escape, but Will blocks his path.

Barbossa, the cursed captain of the *Black Pearl,* plots to retrieve the last piece of the Aztec Gold.

Will enlists the aid of Captain Jack Sparrow to rescue the kidnapped Elizabeth.

Barbossa has the Medallion, but he needs something more—Elizabeth's blood.

Will Turner is in danger. Barbossa needs him to break the curse.

Will and Elizabeth are finally safe . . . and reunited.

Jack faces the gallows. Is this the end for Captain Jack Sparrow?

at anchor in one of the many rocky harbors that lined the island, a light mist rising up around her sides. Inside the captain's cabin, Elizabeth Swann stared out the window at the dark rocks that rose up into the sky. Suddenly, the door swung open and a group of pirates entered, led by Pintel.

"Time to go, poppet," the balding man said gravely.

Once outside, Elizabeth's hands were bound as Barbossa placed the Medallion back around her neck. Despite the damp air and gray skies, Elizabeth did not shiver or cry out. Showing fear would do her no good. These were pirates—they did not care.

Moments later, she found herself sitting in the bow of a longboat being rowed toward a dark cave. In front of her, Barbossa stood in another boat, the cursed monkey on his shoulder and an eager gleam in his eye. They were almost there. Soon, the curse would be over, and he would be a free man once more.

Back aboard the *Interceptor*, an eerie quiet had settled over the crew as they lined up against the rail and stared out into a thick fog. As the ship glided slowly through the water, they could make out the shapes of half-sunken ships. Worn masts rotted in the air, the only sign of the vessels that lay below the waves. Elsewhere, upside-down hulls could be seen, holes worn away in the wood. It was a ship graveyard.

"Puts a chill in the bones," Gibbs said, breaking the silence.

From his spot beside him, Will nodded, his eyes straining for signs of life among the wreckage. Drawing his gaze from the destruction, he turned and looked up to where Jack stood, one hand on the wheel, the other holding his Compass. Cotton, the mute pirate, came up and stood behind him. Feeling the old man's eyes on him, Jack looked back and then snapped the Compass closed.

"How is it that Jack came by that Compass," Will asked Gibbs as the sailor moved off.

Gibbs, never one to turn down the chance to tell a story, looked over toward his captain. "Not a lot's known about Jack Sparrow 'fore he showed up in Tortuga with a mind to go after the treasure of *Isla de Muerta*," he said. "That was back when he was captain of the *Black Pearl*."

"What?" said Will, turning so fast that his

own ponytail almost whipped him in the face. "He failed to mention that."

While Will was bothered by Jack's secrecy, Gibbs knew the man had a reason. When Jack had set out to find the treasure, Gibbs explained to Will, he promised his crew an equal share of the treasure. But they turned on him. As soon as he revealed the bearings, they mutinied, leaving Jack alone on an island . . . to die. But they weren't altogether cruel. They did leave him with a pistol and one bullet.

Gibbs sat down, gesturing for Will to come closer. "But, Jack," he said, when Will was eye level, "he escaped the island. And he still has that single shot. He won't use it though, save on his mutinous first mate."

"Barbossa," Will said, suddenly understanding Jack's eagerness to help him. He hadn't cared about Elizabeth. Jack wanted the *Pearl* . . . and revenge. But he still had one question. "How did Jack get off the island?" he asked.

Gibbs smiled. This was the best part of the story. Gesturing with his hands, he explained, "He roped himself a couple of sea turtles and lashed 'em together and made a raft."

"He roped a couple of sea turtles," Will said

flatly, looking at Gibbs in amusement.

"Aye. Sea turtles."

Leaning closer, Will stared into the older sailor's eyes, not sure who was crazier—Jack or Gibbs. Curious to see if Gibbs could further explain the mystery of Jack's escape, he asked one final question: "What did he use for rope?"

"Human hair," came Jack's voice. "From my back." While Gibbs had been telling Will the story, the captain had made his way over. He now stood glaring down at them, unimpressed. This was no time for storytelling. They had arrived. It was time to go ashore.

As a longboat was readied for Jack and Will. Gibbs jumped up and rushed over to the captain. "What if the worst should happen?" he asked just loud enough for Will to overhear.

"Keep to the Code," Jack ordered.

Without further discussion, Jack and Will slipped into the longboat and headed into the cave—toward Elizabeth and the treasure of *Isla de Muerta*.

Stories told of Isla de Muerta spoke of hidden treasure beyond anyone's imagination. Gold and silver stolen from men and captains too bold to fear ghost stories and pirates. And all the stories were true. Deep inside the island that no man could find if he had not yet been there, a huge treasure lay—sparkling with untold wealth.

The large cavern in which the treasure lay was damp with age and smelled of the saltwater that surrounded it. In the dim light provided by a single hole in the top of the cave and the torch-light they carried, Barbossa's crew could see piles upon piles of gold and colorful treasure.

Sitting on the top of the highest pile of treasure was a single stone chest, its lid pushed aside. It was the chest of Cortés himself. The very same stone chest that had once carried the cursed blood money and which was now filled with eight hundred eighty-one pieces of Aztec Gold—patiently waiting for the last piece.

Barbossa's crew entered and scattered around the cavern, their arms filled with more loot to add to the treasure. They barely even glanced at the large chest. It had long ago ceased to awe them—now it was simply a bane, the cause of their eternal suffering.

While Barbossa's crew was busy with the treasure, Jack and Will were slowly making their way closer. They sat in the longboat, the water illuminated in front of them by the light from the single torch that Jack held in his hand. Rowing the longboat, Will's mind drifted back to Gibbs's question on the *Black Pearl*. "What Code is Gibbs to keep to, if the worst should happen?" he asked Jack.

"Pirates' Code," Jack replied. "Any man who falls behind is left behind."

Suddenly, the cave began to grow brighter, and Will could make out several other longboats moored to a stone shore. They had arrived. Rowing their boat up among the others, Jack and Will jumped out and followed the muffled sound of voices. Moments later, they found themselves looking through a hole into the treasure room. And there, standing behind the large Aztec chest, stood Elizabeth, her head held down by Barbossa's cruel hand.

"Elizabeth," Will said softly, stepping forward. But Jack put out a hand to stop him.

"Not yet," he said quietly. "Wait for the opportune moment."

Glaring at the pirate, Will shrugged off Jack's arm. While he did not often make sense, Jack *did* know these men and this cave. If he said wait, Will would. For now. Will looked through the hole and listened as Barbossa addressed his crew.

"Our torment is near an end!" Barbossa shouted, causing the crew to lift their hands and bellow in agreement. Nodding down at the chest in front of him, he continued. "Here 'tis the cursed treasure of Cortés himself! Every piece that went astray has found its way home—save for this!" Picking up a stone knife, he raised his hand and pointed to the Medallion that lay around Elizabeth's neck. The pirates, sensing that the end of the curse was near, shouted even louder.

From his hiding spot, Will watched as

Barbossa pointed the knife at Elizabeth's throat. His heart pounding, he turned to Jack, only to see him slipping off. Will followed, unwilling to let the captain out of his sight. Sensing that he was being followed, Jack turned. "Listen, squire," he said to Will. "Have I ever given you any reason not to trust me?" Will didn't answer. "Please, stay here and try not to do anything stupid."

Jack walked away, disappearing into the darkness. Meanwhile, Will could hear the shouts of the pirates in the treasure room growing louder. Barbossa was working them into a frenzy. Will did not have much time. With one last look behind him, Will turned and followed Jack back toward the boats. As he passed an oar leaning against the stone wall, he picked it up, causing rocks to skitter down the stone path. Hearing the noise, Jack turned . . . just in time to see an oar swing out and hit him—right across the face. Soundlessly, Jack dropped to the floor. Will leaned over him, holding the oar. "Sorry, Jack," he said to the unconscious man, "but I'm not going to be your leverage."

He turned and ran toward the treasure room to save Elizabeth.

Chapter 16

Elizabeth Swann was beginning to think she might not get out of this particular situation alive. Ever since she had asked for parley and been kidnapped by a crew of cursed pirates, things had gone from bad to worse. Now she stood in a room full of treasure, surrounded by pirates who believed that she was capable of ending the curse and giving them back their lives. As she struggled against Barbossa, she felt his grip tighten around her neck. He shoved her further over the open chest of Aztec Gold. Indeed, things did not look good.

"You know the first thing I'm going to do after the curse is lifted?" Barbossa asked his crew with a grin. Then, answering himself, he said, "Eat a whole bushel of apples."

Grabbing Elizabeth's wrist in his cold hand, Barbossa held it out over the gold and raised his knife. Elizabeth turned her head away, closing her eyes as she prepared for the cut. She felt the blade on her palm and then a brief stab of pain. Opening her eyes, she looked down and watched as Barbossa placed the Medallion over the small cut on her hand. Closing her fist, he waited, allowing her blood to touch the gold. "Begun by blood, by blood undone," he said. Then, forcing open her palm, he dropped the gold.

With bated breath, Barbossa, Elizabeth, and the crew watched as it fell into the chest with the matching pieces. For a few moments, the room was silent as the pirates waited for something to happen.

"I don't feel no different," Ragetti said, speaking for the group.

"How do we tell?" Pintel asked.

From his spot by the chest, Barbossa frowned. It was true. Something did not feel right. While there was no guarantee that the curse's undoing would be dramatic, he had expected some sort of change. Drawing his pistol, he aimed it at Pintel and fired, hitting the stocky man in the center of his chest.

Grabbing his chest in shock, Pintel looked

down, waiting for the blood that should follow. But no blood came. The curse had not been broken. Angry shouts and cries rose up, and the men's stormy glares fixed on Elizabeth.

"You," Barbossa snarled, grabbing up the Medallion and shoving it in her face. "Your father. Was your father William Turner?"

"No," Elizabeth answered.

"Where's his child?" asked Barbossa. "The child in whose veins flows the blood of William Turner?"

When Elizabeth did not answer, Barbossa slapped her, sending her, and the Medallion, flying down the pile of gold. She landed, unconscious, on a ledge of gems. To one side, a deep stream of seawater flowed, and as she fell, pieces of treasure slipped off the ledge and disappeared into the dark water.

With the girl out of the way, Barbossa turned back to his angry crew. The situation was getting dangerously out of control. "You two," shouted the Bo'sun, pointing at Pintel and Ragetti, "you brought us the wrong person!"

"She had the medallion!" argued Pintel.

"She said her name was Turner!" Ragetti added.

From his spot in the angry crowd, Twigg, the tall pirate who had had a run-in with Jack in the jail earlier, came forward. His expression was murderous as he stared at Barbossa. "You," he snarled. "It's you who brought us here in the first place."

As the accusations continued to fly, no one bothered to keep an eye on Elizabeth. Lying on the ledge, her eyes slowly opened and she tried to lift her head. Suddenly, a hand reached out and covered her mouth. It was Will! While the pirates had been busy attacking one another, he had slipped into the water and made his way to Elizabeth's side. Now, he gestured at the exit and started to pull her toward the water. Shaking her head, she nodded back at the Medallion that lay close by. Silently, she crept over, picked it up, and then slipped, unnoticed, into the water beside Will.

Barbossa, meanwhile, was trying to regain order over his crew. "Any more talk," he shouted, "and I'll chain ye all to a cannon and send ye to the watery depths!"

Suddenly, Barbossa's monkey began to jump up and down, screeching for all it was worth.

Barbossa turned, his eyes flying from the frantic monkey to the spot where Elizabeth was supposed to be—but wasn't. With a roar of rage, he looked over in time to see Elizabeth and Will's figures retreating to the safety of the longboats. "The Medallion!" he shouted. "She's taken it!"

Scrambling into action, the pirates headed for the longboats. But when they arrived, they encountered a minor problem—all the oars were missing! Letting out a collective scream of rage, the crew scurried to find anything in the treasure room that could be used as an oar.

Close by, a dazed Jack Sparrow was coming to. In one hand, he held the oar with which Will had so unkindly smashed, while his other hand was pressed to his aching head.

"You!" said Ragetti, when his eyes landed on his old captain. "You're supposed to be dead!"

"I'm not?" Jack asked, utterly confused by the situation in which he now found himself. Last time he checked, he was sneaking away from Will, with a plan to get the *Black Pearl* back . . . sort of. Now he was surrounded by an angry mob of cursed pirates, and his head ached to high heaven.

Making matters worse, Pintel suddenly drew his pistol and aimed it at Jack's chest. He had to do something quickly, or, unlike the other pirates, he would be quite dead. "Par . . . Pas . . ." he stuttered, trying to say the one word he knew could help him. "Par . . . parsnip? No . . . parsley? Ah, parley. Yes, parley."

With a groan, the pirates lowered their weapons.

"Parley!" cried Pintel. "Curses to the depths whatever muttonhead thought up parley!"

As they led Jack away from the water and back to a waiting Barbossa, he leaned over to Pintel. "That would be the French," he said, a smile on his lips.

Will Turner threw the last of the pirates' oars overboard and climbed onto the deck of the *Interceptor.* Streaming out behind him in a long line were the rest of the oars that he and Elizabeth had taken when they escaped the cave. Now, the two of them stood dripping in front of a crew of very confused looking shipmates.

"Where be Jack?" asked Gibbs.

Elizabeth started at the mention of the notorious pirate. Had he been involved in her escape? The same man who had used her to get away from the Royal Navy had come to rescue her? It seemed very unlikely. But now this man that she quickly recognized as the grouchy sailor Gibbs, whom she had met eight years ago, was asking for his whereabouts.

"He fell behind," Will answered, not meeting the man's eye, as Anamaria gave the orders and the crew prepared to sail. The Code left them no options. They were to leave Jack.

Meanwhile, Jack Sparrow was attempting to negotiate his way out of a very sticky situation. Having no way to escape from *Isla de Muerta,* seeing as all the oars for the longboats had somehow upped and gone, he now found himself face-to-face with his old first mate and current enemy—Barbossa.

"How the blazes did you get off that island?" Barbossa asked upon seeing Jack.

Jack flashed his trademark grin, but his eyes remained cold and guarded. "When you marooned me on that spit of land," he said slowly, "you forgot one very important thing, mate. I'm Captain Jack Sparrow."

"Ah," said Barbossa. "Then I won't be making that mistake again. Gents—kill him."

The crew happily cocked their pistols.

But Jack held up a hand. "The girl's blood didn't work, did it?" he asked.

Barbossa snapped to attention. Leave it to Jack Sparrow to get the upper hand. "You know whose blood we need?" Barbossa asked.

Jack leveled his eyes with Barbossa's, a

knowing gleam flashing between them. "I know whose blood you need."

Meanwhile, back in a cabin on the *Interceptor*, Elizabeth Swann sat and attempted to bandage her wounded hand. It still stung from where the blade had sliced into her palm, but the bleeding had lessened.

Will Turner sat across from Elizabeth, his forehead etched with worry as he watched her fumble with the white gauze. Reaching out, he took her hand in his and slowly began to redo the wrapping. For a few moments, there was silence as the two gazed intently at their hands.

Finally, Will broke the silence. "You gave Barbossa my name as yours," he said. "Why?"

"I don't know," she answered, looking up and meeting his gaze. The searching look in her eyes caused Will to pull the gauze too tightly, and Elizabeth let out a little cry.

"I'm sorry—blacksmith's hands."

But that did not seem to bother Elizabeth. She began to lean forward, knowing that what she wanted to say would be done best without words.

Sensing what was about to happen, Will,

too, leaned forward. But instead of the kiss he had expected, he felt something cool pressed into his palm. Looking down, his eyes came to rest on a gold medallion.

"It's yours," Elizabeth explained.

Suddenly, Will remembered. "It was a gift . . . from my father. Why did you take it?" he asked.

"I was afraid you were a pirate," she said.

Understanding flooded through Will. It all made sense now. Elizabeth had told the pirates her name was Turner. Jack had mentioned that Will's father was Bootstrap Bill—a pirate. Therefore, the pirates had believed they held a pirate's child captive. "It wasn't your blood they needed," he said aloud. "It was my father's blood. My blood. The blood of a pirate."

Onboard the *Black Pearl*, Jack Sparrow found himself back where he belonged—in the captain's cabin attempting to reach an accord with Barbossa. Unfortunately, since he had last been in the room, the place had fallen into a sorry state of affairs. Sitting at the large dining table that filled most of the room, he glanced at the tattered fixtures. Pity, he thought, that such a fine ship should have become so neglected.

"You expect to leave me standing on some beach with nothing more than a name and your word it's the one we need," the cursed captain was saying, "and watch you sail away on my ship?"

Reaching over to pull a green apple from the bowl in front of him, Jack turned his attention back to Barbossa. "Oh, no," he said. "I expect to leave you standing on some beach with absolutely no name at all, watching me sail away on my ship—and then I'll shout the name back to you, savvy?" Smiling, he took a bite out of the juicy apple and watched as Barbossa squirmed.

As he jealously watched Jack chew the apple, Barbossa pointed out that the plan required trusting Jack's word—not something he was inclined to do given their history.

But, as Jack pointed out, of the two of them, only Barbossa had taken part in a mutiny. So, really, it was Jack's word that they should be trusting. Then, as an afterthought, he added, "Although I should be thanking you. If you hadn't betrayed me and left me to die, I'd have had an equal share in the curse."

They were interrupted by the Bo'sun, who

appeared at the door with news. The *Interceptor* was in sight. Without a word, the pair headed for the main deck. Pulling out a spyglass, Barbossa focused in on the *Interceptor*. She was making good speed, but she was no match for the *Black Pearl*. Suddenly, Jack's face blocked Barbossa's view.

"I'm having a thought here," he interjected. "We run up a flag of truce, I go over and negotiate the return of your Medallion. What say you to that?"

Barbossa brought the spyglass down and glared at the wily pirate. He was always negotiating—and plotting. But Barbossa knew better.

"Now, Jack. That's exactly the attitude that lost you the *Pearl*. Bodies are easier to search when they're dead."

Turning, Barbossa ordered Jack to the brig. He would deal with him later. Now he needed to get to that ship . . . and the Medallion.

Chapter 18

Aboard the *Interceptor,* Elizabeth Swann was just emerging onto the deck. She had left Will below, unsure of what to say to him now that she had given him the Medallion. Looking around, she noticed that the crew was frantically running about as Gibbs and Anamaria shouted orders.

"What's happening?" she asked, running over to Gibbs. Following his gaze, Elizabeth gasped. There, on the horizon, surrounded by a thick fog, was the *Black Pearl*—and she was gaining. If they were to escape Barbossa's clutches, they would have to act fast.

Turning her attention back to Gibbs and Anamaria, Elizabeth said, "We've got a shallower draft, right?" At Anamaria's nod, she continued. "Then can't we lose them among the shoals?"

The three turned and looked to the horizon in front of them. Not far away, the indistinct shape of a rocky outcropping could be seen.

Apparently thinking that Elizabeth's idea was better than no idea, Anamaria turned to the crew and barked out new orders. "Lighten the ship! Stem to stern!"

Barbossa, however, had no intention of letting them get away. With Jack safely locked below, Barbossa watched as the crew of the *Interceptor* began to throw cargo overboard. He had them running scared!

"Raise the flag, and run out the guns!" he ordered. "Haul on the mainsails and let go!" From the side of the *Black Pearl*, oars appeared and the crew began to row, adding to the ship's already increasing speed. And from the mainsail, a flag unfurled, revealing the black-and-white skull and crossbones of the Jolly Roger.

Walking onto the *Interceptor*'s deck, Will, too, took in the chaos and looked behind him just in time to see the Jolly Roger begin to snap in the air. Running over to the rail, he grabbed a line and watched as the *Pearl*'s oars appeared. All around him, the crew continued to throw whatever they could overboard. Just in time, he stopped two men from throwing a cannon into the water—that, they definitely were going to need.

But despite their efforts, the *Black Pearl* continued to gain on them. Acting quickly, Will ordered the crew to load the remaining guns with whatever they could find—silverware, nails, even glass. As long as it could be fired, it would do. Now, they just needed to find a way to get the *Pearl* along their port side—facing the cannons. Turning once again to Anamaria, Elizabeth shouted, "Drop the anchor starboard side!"

"You're daft, lady!" Anamaria shouted back, but she saw that the *Pearl* was now even closer and within moments would be in firing range. There was no time to argue. With a splash, the anchor dropped into the blue water and began to drag along the bottom. Hooking on a reef, the anchor line pulled taut, and with a loud groan the *Interceptor* began to pivot, her bow almost pulled underwater by the motion. Below decks, anything not nailed down slid across the floor—including the gold Medallion. Sliding across the table, it fell to the ground with a clank.

When the ship finally stopped pivoting,

there was a moment of odd silence as both crews evaluated the situation. The *Black Pearl* and the *Interceptor* now sat parallel to each other—at the ready for a fight.

At almost the exact same moment, "Fire!" rang out from both ships, and the air filled with the sound of cannons blasting. For several agonizing moments, the blue sky turned gray with smoke, and screams could be heard across the water. When the smoke finally cleared and the guns were silenced, everyone took in the damage. Steaming holes gaped from the side of the *Interceptor*'s hull, while over on the *Pearl*, silverware and glass littered the deck and hull. Near one of the *Pearl*'s cannons, Pintel and Ragetti looked out at the other ship. Looking over at his friend, Pintel noticed that the man had a fork sticking out of his wooden eye. Yanking it out, the skinny one-eyed pirate shook his head. Blasted cannons!

Still locked in the *Black Pearl*'s brig, Jack peered through a hole in the ship and watched as the cannons fired. Suddenly a blast rang out and Jack ducked just as a huge hole was blown through his cell wall. "Stop blowing holes in my ship!" he cried out.

Then something caught his eye. Jack's luck had just taken another decidedly positive turn—the door to his cell had been blasted open. He was free. Skipping through the water, he pushed open the door further and made his way out. It was time to take back the *Pearl*.

As Barbossa continued to lay siege to the *Interceptor*, Elizabeth, Will, Gibbs, and Anamaria desperately tried to think of a new plan.

"We need us a devil's dowry," Gibbs said hopelessly.

"We've got one!" shouted Anamaria, grabbing Elizabeth. "We'll give 'im her!"

But Will knew that Elizabeth was worth nothing to Barbossa. The cursed pirate would not stop the fight until he had something far smaller and of much more value—the Medallion.

Without another word, Will turned and headed belowdecks. If Barbossa wanted the Medallion, he would get the Medallion. Will had almost lost Elizabeth once—he would not lose her again.

The fight was in full force as Will went belowdecks in search of the Medallion. Back aboard the *Black Pearl,* Barbossa shouted orders to his men, eager to get what he was looking for and then head back to *Isla de Muerta.*

Suddenly, with a loud creak, the mast of the *Interceptor* snapped, sending it crashing down. Fallen, the long piece of wood created a bridge between the two ships. Seeing his chance, Barbossa ordered his men to board the *Interceptor.* "Find me that Medallion." he shouted.

Jack, meanwhile, had snuck unnoticed onto the deck. As men hurried across the fallen mast and grabbed lines to swing over the water, Jack waited for his chance. One of the men, missing his landing, swung back over the water and dropped into the waves below. Grabbing the now free rope, Jack tipped his hat. "Thanks very much," he said to the man in the water below before he took hold and swung across. Upon landing, Jack scanned the deck. Spotting Elizabeth, he rushed over. "Where's the Medallion?" he asked, grabbing her by the shoulders.

In response, she reached out to slap him. But Jack had learned his lesson on Tortuga. Grabbing her wrist, he noticed the bandaged hand and the look of fury in her eyes. "Ah," he sighed. "And where is dear William, then?"

The look of anger vanished as a realization dawned on Elizabeth. Will had gone belowdecks and not returned.

As water rose steadily below the decks of the damaged *Interceptor,* Will searched in vain for the Medallion. Pieces of wood and debris floated past as his hands searched the water for any sign of the gold. Hearing a screech, he looked up to see the cursed monkey standing at a hole in the bulkhead. In the creature's hand was the Medallion. With one last screech, it turned and leaped outside, leaving Will alone in the rising water.

Rushing over to the door to the bulkhead,

Will pushed against it, but it would not budge. It was blocked. Seeing the futility in trying to get out that way, he swam toward a grate that opened to the deck while the water continued to rise. On the other side, he heard Elizabeth call his name and then she was there, reaching her fingers toward him.

"Elizabeth," he said, desperation in his voice. Then, as he watched helplessly, two pirates grabbed her by the shoulders and dragged her away. A moment later, his fingers slipped down as he disappeared beneath the water.

As Will was claimed by the sea and Elizabeth was dragged away by the cursed pirates, Jack saw his last bargaining chip being carried back toward the *Black Pearl* in the hands of a monkey. The Medallion glittered in the sunlight as the creature scampered over the mast. Taking off after it, Jack shimmied across the mast, using his hands to balance. On the other side, he reached out to grab the Medallion, but it was too late. Another hand had reached out first.

Bringing his gaze up, Jack's eyes landed on Barbossa. "Why, thank you, Jack!" the man said.

"You're welcome," Jack replied.

"Not you. We named the monkey Jack." Turning, Barbossa raised the Medallion and addressed his crew. "Gents," he shouted, "our hope is restored."

A short while later, the crew of the *Interceptor* found themselves tied to the *Black Pearl*'s mast. Holding the Medallion in his fingertips, Barbossa waited, while Pintel pointed his gun at the captives. "Any of you so much as thinks the word 'parley,' I'll have your guts for garters."

Tied up with the crew, Elizabeth stared over at the *Interceptor*. Fires burned over the hull, and the remaining sails were ripped and torn. And somewhere onboard, Elizabeth believed, was her beloved Will.

Pushing the ropes up and over her head, she slipped free and moved forward. But before she had taken even two steps, the *Interceptor* exploded, sending debris high into the air. "Will!" Elizabeth shouted, rushing to the rail. With rage in her eyes, she attacked Barbossa.

Grabbing her by the wrists, Barbossa just laughed. "Welcome back, miss. You took advantage of our hospitality last time. It holds fair now you return the favor." With another laugh, he shoved her at a group of dirty pirates who began to hoot and jeer.

But they were interrupted by a shout. "Barbossa!"

Climbing up onto the rail, his clothes soaking wet, was Will Turner. At Elizabeth's excited shout, he gave her an almost imperceptible nod before jumping off the rail and grabbing Jack's pistol, which lay on a table of loot nearby. "She goes free," he demanded, walking to Barbossa and cocking the pistol.

"What's in your head, boy?" Barbossa asked, unbothered by Will's dramatic appearance. "You've only got one shot—and we can't die."

Jack Sparrow, standing off to one side, shook his head. "Don't do anything stupid," he muttered to Will.

But it was too late. Raising the pistol, Will stepped back onto the rail and pointed it at his own head. "You can't. I can."

Seeing that he would have to step in and defuse the situation—or at least try to keep Will from ruining his plans—Jack spoke up. "He's no one," he explained, dismissively. "A distant cousin of my aunt's nephew once removed."

Ignoring Jack, Will went on. "My name is Will Turner. My father was Bootstrap Bill Turner. His blood runs in my veins."

Murmurs of understanding began to ripple among the crew as Will's words sunk in.

"Name your terms, Mr. *Turner*," Barbossa said.

Glancing over at Elizabeth, Will demanded that she and the crew go free. He neglected, however, to mention Jack Sparrow. From his spot on the deck, Jack sighed. Try and help a man out and what does he do? Stab you in the back. Young Mr. Turner was turning into quite a pirate.

Elizabeth Swann, her dark dress billowing in the ocean breeze, stood on a plank over the blue Caribbean Sea. Behind her, Will struggled against the ropes that held him, his eyes flashing with anger as he tried to call out. But it was no use. He was bound and gagged, helpless, as he watched Elizabeth walk to her "freedom."

Barbossa had gotten what he needed—the Medallion and the blood. As for his promises?

Well, they were open to interpretation. After giving Will his word that Elizabeth would go free, he had set course back to *Isla de Muerta*—with one stop on the way.

Now, the *Black Pearl* sat off the shore of a small island that was nothing more than a strip of beach and a few palm trees. Turning his attention back to Elizabeth, Barbossa ordered her off the plank. But not without first asking for his dress back. Scowling, she ripped it off and threw it at him. "Here!" she said, trying to sound braver as she stood shivering in her shift. "It goes well with your black heart!" With one last look at Will, she moved to the end of the plank and fell into the water below.

Jack Sparrow, his hands tied in front of him, was next. "I really hoped we were past all this," he said.

Walking over, Barbossa flung an arm around the man's shoulders and smiled, his teeth brown in the sun. "Jack, Jack . . . Now, didn't you notice," he said. "That's the same little island we made you governor of on our last little trip. Perhaps you'll be able to conjure up another miraculous escape." Pausing, he added, "But I doubt it."

Pulling out his sword, he urged Jack further out onto the plank. Time was wasting. There were curses to be *un*done and living to be done.

But Jack wasn't ready to jump quite yet. "Last time you left me a pistol, with one shot," he pointed out. When Barbossa produced Jack's pistol, the pirate tried his luck one more time. "Seeing as there's two of us, a gentlman would give us two pistols."

"It'll be one pistol, as before," Barbossa replied. "And you can be the gentlman an' shoot the lady and starve to death yourself." Taking Jack's effects, he threw them with a splash into the water. A moment later there was another splash as Jack dove in after them.

Stumbling onto the white sand that surrounded the tiny strip of an island, Elizabeth and Jack turned and watched as the *Black Pearl* faded into the horizon.

Loosening the rope around his hands, Jack squinted in the sun and sighed. "That's the second time I've had to watch that man sail away with my ship," he said. Then, turning, he strode off, leaving a hopeless Elizabeth in his wake.

Watching Captain Jack Sparrow sashay away from the shore, Elizabeth Swann clenched her fists. She would not let him get away so easily. His pirating ways had landed them in this mess and now they would help get them out of it. With one last glance behind her, Elizabeth took off after him.

"But you were marooned on this same island before," she shouted as she caught up to Jack. "We can get off the same way you did then!"

The sound of Elizabeth's voice grated on Jack—as did her naïveté. Whirling around, he stood and glared at her, the red of his bandanna gleaming in the sunshine.

"To what point and purpose?" he asked. "The *Black Pearl* is gone. And unless you have a rudder and a lot of sails hidden in that bodice . . ." He paused and leaned back a bit as his eyes moved up and down Elizabeth. Then he added, "Young Mr. Turner will be dead long before you reach him."

He began to stride away, his steps exaggerated as he counted under his breath. Undeterred by the pirate's erratic behavior, Elizabeth continued to follow him, talking as she went. "But you're *Captain* Jack Sparrow! You vanished from under the noses of seven agents of the East India Trading Company!" Elizabeth reached out and grabbed Jack by the shoulders, turning him around so that she could stare directly into his brown eyes as she added, "Are you the pirate I've read about or not? How did you escape last time?"

For a moment, Jack seemed uncertain of what to say. The girl's interest and knowledge of him was quite flattering, but she did not have the whole story. Sighing, he confessed. "Last time," he said, stomping on the sandy ground, "I was here a grand total of three days." As he continued to speak, he pushed her backward and leaned down. Then, with a grunt, he leaned over and pushed aside sand, revealing a trapdoor. Pulling it up, he quickly descended the staircase and disappeared. His voice was muffled as he continued to speak. "Last time the rumrunners who used this island as a cache came by, and I bartered passage off."

Suddenly, from the hole, Jack's hand emerged, an old bottle of rum clenched tightly in his fingers. Elizabeth's eyes grew wide as the truth of Jack's so-called adventure sunk in. "So that's it?" she said in exasperation. "You spent three days lying on the beach drinking rum?"

Back above ground, Jack held out another bottle of rum to Elizabeth and shrugged. "Welcome to the Caribbean, love," he said, popping the cork of his own bottle and tilting his head back.

Beneath a starry sky, Elizabeth and Jack, arms linked, danced around a large fire with their rum bottles in hand. Their voices echoed off the empty sea as they sang a familiar pirate shanty. Dropping to the ground, Elizabeth dragged Jack down beside her. Her disappointment at learning Jack's true story had faded with the day—and now she was content to drink, sing, and dance. . . .

"When I get the *Pearl* back," Jack said, his

tone sounding quite serious, despite the bottle in his hand, "I'm going to teach that song to the whole crew, and we'll sing it all the time!"

"You'll be positively the most fearsome pirates to sail the Spanish Main," Elizabeth shouted.

For a moment, Jack considered the possibility. In the light from the fire, his brown eyes looked almost kind. "Not just the Spanish Main," he told Elizabeth. "The whole world . . . Wherever we want to go, we go. That's what a ship is, you know. Not just a keel and a hull and a deck and sails. That's what a ship needs. But what a ship is—what the *Black Pearl* really is—is freedom." With a sigh, Jack turned toward the sea, lost in thoughts of his ship.

Despite herself, Elizabeth momentarily felt her heart flutter. In his voice, Elizabeth could hear Jack's pain. While he swaggered about with a supreme air of confidence that Elizabeth often found infuriating, there was another side of him—a softer side. Leaning down, she rested her head on his shoulder and sighed. This new side of Jack was going to make what she did next a bit harder. "Jack," she said softly, "it must really be terrible for you to be trapped on this island."

However, at the moment, Jack was not at all opposed to being trapped. Unlike his last visit, he now had company. And, he realized, looking down at Elizabeth's porcelain skin and brown eyes, said company was quite easy on the eyes. Raising his arm slowly, he brought it around Elizabeth's back and rested a hand on her shoulder.

Shaking off his hand, Elizabeth raised her bottle. "To freedom," she said, pretending to take a swig.

"To the *Black Pearl,*" added Jack, unaware of Elizabeth's ruse. Then, tilting his head back he began to swallow until, with one last gulp, he fell back into the sand, unconscious. Elizabeth had knocked Jack out cold.

The smell of fire filtered through Jack's nose, and with effort he opened one eye and tried to take in his surroundings. He was still on the beach near the remains of the bonfire, but the stars were gone, replaced by a brilliant blue, cloudless sky. But the smoke? It wasn't coming from the fire he had built the previous night. Suddenly, a loud explosion rocked the island. That was *definitely* not coming from the bonfire. Sitting up quickly,

Jack groaned and placed a hand on his aching head. What he saw when his blurry eyes focused made his head ache even more. Elizabeth Swann, her white dressing gown covered in soot, raced around a patch of palm trees, throwing barrels of rum into an already billowing fire. As they landed in the heat, the barrels exploded, sending splinters of wood flying high into the air.

"No!" shouted Jack, scrambling to his feet and placing his hands on either side of his head. "Not good! Stop! You've burned all the food, the shade—the rum!"

"Yes," Elizabeth shouted back as she continued to fuel the fire. "The rum is gone."

"But why is the rum gone?" Jack asked.

Turning her back on the flames, Elizabeth walked over to Jack. "That signal," she said, pointing to the fire, "goes up a thousand feet. The entire Royal Navy is out looking for me. Do you think there is even the slightest chance they won't see it?" At Jack's groan, Elizabeth raised her chin proudly and added, "Just wait, Captain Sparrow. In an hour, maybe two, there'll be white sails on that horizon."

Without another word, she plopped down

on the sand and wrapped her arms around her knees. Grabbing the pistol from his belt, Jack struggled to remain calm. The rum was gone. The shade was gone. And this little, aggravating fool thought she was so smart. Shaking with the effort to not use his last bullet on Elizabeth, Jack turned and stalked off, muttering under his breath.

A few minutes later, Jack crested a dune, still trying to put as much distance as he could between himself and Elizabeth. Looking out to sea, he did a double take. There, on the horizon, her white sails billowing, was the HMS *Dauntless*.

Sighing, Jack looked back toward where Elizabeth sat. "There'll be no living with her after this," he murmured.

Chapter 21

Safely back aboard the HMS *Dauntless*, Elizabeth Swann found herself once again butting heads with a stubborn man. But this time, the man was not the infamous Captain Jack Sparrow. It was Commodore Norrington.

"We have to go back," she shouted at him. "We have to rescue Will!"

Governor Swann, who had chosen to accompany the commodore as he searched for Elizabeth, stepped forward. Unlike Elizabeth and Jack, who both wore a fine layer of dirt, gun powder, and rum smoke on their skin, the governor looked dapper and clean. The curls of his white wig hung just so and there was only the smallest touch of worry in his eyes. After all, Elizabeth was now safe and the pirate Jack Sparrow stood captive between two marines, his ankles in chains. There was no need to complicate matters by worrying over the life of a young blacksmith. "The boy's fate is regrettable," he said, when Elizabeth accused him of condemning Will to death. "But so was his decision to engage in piracy."

The decision had been made. The *Dauntless* would return to Port Royal, Jack Sparrow would hang, and the rest of them would continue on with their lives.

From his spot on the rail, Jack Sparrow listened quietly. An idea was forming in his head. Reaching up, he twirled his goatee in his fingers.

"If I may be so bold to interject my professional opinion," he said, stepping away from the two marines and shuffling toward the commodore and governor, the metal around his ankles clanking. Holding his hands up, he said, "The *Pearl* was listing near to scuppers after the battle. Very unlikely she'll make good time. Think about it, Commodore—the *Black Pearl* . . . the last real pirate threat in the Caribbean, mate. How can you pass that up?"

But apparently, Norrington could and would pass up the chance to capture the *Black Pearl*. Turning, he began to walk back toward the helm, only to be stopped by Elizabeth's voice.

"Commodore," she said. "I beg you—please do this . . . for me. As a wedding gift."

Slowly, Norrington turned and looked at Elizabeth, unable to speak. Governor Swann, on the other hand, was quite capable of speech. Rushing over to his daughter's side, he placed a hand on her shoulder. "My dear," he said with excitement, "are you accepting the commodore's proposal?"

"I am," she replied.

At Elizabeth's affirmation, Jack began to jump up and down. "A wedding!" he said. "I love weddings!"

Jack's outburst was just what Norrington needed to propel him back into action. With one last glance at Elizabeth, Norrington strode toward Jack, stopping mere inches from his face. "Mister Sparrow," he said in a clipped tone. "You will accompany these men to the helm and provide them with a bearing to *Isla de Muerta*. Do I make myself clear?"

"Inescapably," Jack replied, trying not to smile. He had gotten what he wanted, after all—they were going back for the *Black Pearl*.

* * *

While the HMS *Dauntless* changed course and began to head to *Isla de Muerta*, the *Black Pearl* was already well on her way. In the brig below-decks, the surviving members of Jack's crew from the destroyed *Interceptor* stood and watched as Pintel and Ragetti mopped the floors.

Will Turner, in a separate cell, paced back and forth, his mind racing. Suddenly, he stopped and rested his arm on the cell bars. "You knew William Turner," he asked Pintel, the closer of the two pirates.

Pausing mid-mop, Pintel looked up and sighed. His bald head reflected the dim light from the lanterns along the walls and his eyes were cold. But still, he answered. "Ol' Bootstrap Bill? We knew him."

As Ragetti continued to mop, Pintel added, "It never sat well with Bootstrap what we did to Jack Sparrow—the mutiny and all. Said it wasn't right with the Code. That's why he sent off a piece of the treasure—said we deserved to remain cursed."

As Pintel continued to talk, Will lowered his head. His father was a man who knew right from wrong and who had made these pirates pay.

He was a good man. And a pirate. Will had spent all his life hating pirates. But now? Now everything had changed.

Pintel continued his tale of Bootstrap. "So what Captain Barbossa did, he strapped a cannon to Bootstrap's bootstraps and the last we saw, he was sinking to the crushing black oblivion of Davy Jones's Locker." At the mention of Davy Jones, there was moment of silence. Then, Pintel added, "It was only after that we learned we needed his blood to lift the curse."

Suddenly, the sound of footsteps echoed through the brig and Barbossa appeared. "Bring him," he ordered, nodding in the direction of Will.

They had arrived at *Isla de Muerta*. It was time to end the curse once and for all.

Through the lens of his spyglass, Commodore Norrington stared out at the *Black Pearl*. Hidden among the rocks that lined *Isla de Muerta*, two of the *Dauntless*'s longboats floated gently in the water. Norrington sat at the head of the lead boat, his spyglass in hand, while behind him sat Jack, closely guarded by Murtogg and Mullroy—

the same two dimwitted marines the pirate had encountered back in Port Royal.

"I don't care for the situation," Norrington said, lowering his spyglass. The deck of the *Black Pearl* appeared empty. The only sign of life was a lantern or two rocking in the gentle ocean breeze. "Any attempt to storm the island could turn into an ambush."

"Not if you do the ambushing," Jack pointed out, moving closer to the commodore. While the pirate had successfully managed to get back to *Isla de Muerta*, there was still the matter of getting his ship back. And in order to do *that*, he would need to be in control of the situation—without anyone's knowledge of course. When Norrington did not immediately shut him up, Jack continued. "I'll go in and convince Barbossa to send his men out—leaving you to do nothing but blast them silly with your cannons."

Norrington paused to consider Jack's suggestion. While he hated to admit it, the pirate's plan was not entirely without merit. Nodding, he agreed. If Jack wanted to go in after the murderous Barbossa, Norrrington would not stand in his way.

At the commodore's nod, Jack smiled.

Things were working out perfectly. There was just one more thing he had to take care of—keeping Elizabeth quiet about the curse.

"Now, to be quite honest" he added, once more getting Norrington's attention by tapping him on the shoulder. "There's a risk to those aboard the *Dauntless*, which includes the future Mrs. Commodore. . . ."

Moments later, Elizabeth Swann found herself being dragged unceremoniously toward the captain's cabin—for her own "safety." Struggling against the men, she tried to explain that the pirates they were going after were cursed. But it was no use—the officers just laughed at her.

As the door shut behind her, she sighed in frustration. This was all Jack Sparrow's doing.

And out on the water, rowing swiftly away from the *Dauntless*, Jack Sparrow smiled. The *Black Pearl* was as good as his.

Inside *Isla de Muerta,* the cave of treasure suddenly filled with light as Barbossa and his men entered with their torches. Will Turner was shoved into the room by Pintel and Ragetti, his hands tied behind his back and the gold Medallion around his neck.

"No reason to fret," Pintel said with a laugh. "It's just a prick of the finger and a few drops of blood."

But the pirate Twigg had another idea. "There'll be no mistakes this time. We spill it all."

It appeared Will actually did have reason to worry. As he was shoved forward, Will felt his hope begin to slip away. It would take a miracle to get out of this situation—and he seemed to be plum out of miracles.

A few moments later, the cave filled with the shouts of the pirates as the moment of truth drew nearer. Torchlight flickered off the cave walls and mixed with the moonlight filtering down from a hole above, adding an eerie ambience to the event. Hunched over the open chest of Aztec Gold, Will looked out at the frenzied pirates and groaned. Barbossa, standing close beside Will, held up a knife and listened as the shouts increased.

Suddenly, Barbossa caught a movement in the crowd and saw the flash of a familiar red bandanna.

"Excuse me. Pardon me . . . ah, begun by blood."

"Jack!" Will shouted when the pirate finally pushed and sashayed his way to the front of the crowd.

"Not possible," Barbossa hissed. He had left Jack to die on that island—again. And again, the rascally man had somehow managed to escape. It was clear that this man was more of a curse to Barbossa than the one caused by the Aztec Gold.

Jack lifted a finger. "Not probable," he pointed out.

"Where's Elizabeth?" Will asked, staring

Jack in the eye and shrugging off the hands that held him over the chest.

"She's safe, just like I promised," Jack assured, before adding that she had promised to marry Norrington and that, of course, Will had promised to die for her. So they were all good on their promises. When Jack finally finished his explanation, Barbossa threw up his hands. He didn't have time for this.

"Shut up!" he shouted, pointing his knife at Jack. "You're next."

As Jack recoiled, Barbossa turned and shoved Will back down over the chest. Holding his knife against the boy's throat, he prepared to cut.

But once again, Jack interrupted. "You don't want to be doing that," he said.

"No," Barbossa replied. "I really think I do."

Shrugging, Jack clasped his hands together and began to examine the slippery rocks around him. "All right," he said, appearing thoroughly intrigued by his surroundings. "It's your funeral." When Barbossa finally asked why, Jack looked up and began to take a step forward.

"Well," he explained, "because the HMS

Dauntless, pride of the Royal Navy, is floating just offshore . . . waiting for you."

As the pirates began to murmur and groan, Jack smiled. He had Barbossa and his men just where he wanted them.

Floating safely outside the cave was the crew of the *Dauntless*, but they were not aboard their ship. Instead, the majority of the crew sat floating in seven longboats, preparing for attack. Sitting among his men, Commodore Norrington kept a lookout for any sign of movement, while behind him Murtogg and Mullroy argued back and forth.

"What are we doing here?" whispered Murtogg.

Rolling his eyes at Murtogg's apparent stupidity, Mullroy replied, "The pirates come out, unprepared and unawares—we catch 'em in a crossfire and send 'em down to sea."

From his spot at the front of the longboat, Norrington smiled. Let Jack Sparrow think he was calling all the shots. It would only make victory all the sweeter when Jack, *along* with Barbossa and his crew, was caught in a trap of his own making.

* * *

Back in the cave, Captain Jack Sparrow was negotiating . . . yet again. Having caught Barbossa's attention with news of the looming attack, he was now hoping to put the last of his plan into action. But he needed to convince Barbossa to attack first. The other captain stood with his knife still in hand while Jack began to speak. Will, from his spot nearby listened closely, interested to see what Jack Sparrow had to say this time around.

"So you order your men to row out to the *Dauntless*, and they do what they do best," Jack began, "and there you are! With two ships. The makings of your very own fleet. Of course, you'll take the grandest as your flagship, but what of the *Pearl*?" Stopping, Jack waited and watched as Barbossa's eyes began to twinkle. When Jack was sure he had Barbossa dreaming of a fleet at his command, he made one more suggestion. "Name me captain. I sail under your colors, I give you ten percent of my plunder, and you get to introduce yourself as Commodore Barbossa, savvy?"

Commodore Barbossa. It had a nice ring to it. While he was more inclined to simply lock up Jack and continue on with killing young Mr. Turner, there was something appealing about having his own fleet. But there had to be a catch.

"I suppose in exchange, you want me not to kill the whelp," he said, nodding at Will.

"Not at all. By all means, kill the whelp," Jack said casually, reaching down and picking up a handful of coins from the chest.

Will, helpless to do anything, glared at the pirate. He had been right not to trust Jack all along. But, as Will watched, Jack looked over at him and widened his eyes. Turning back to Barbossa, Jack added, "Wait to lift the curse until the opportune moment. For instance: after you've killed Norrington's men. Every . . . last . . . one of them." One by one he dropped the coins back into the chest, the clink of gold hitting gold emphasizing Jack's words. Only Will, curious after hearing the pirate use the familiar phrase, saw him slyly slip one coin up into the billowing sleeves of his shirt.

"You've been planning this all along," Will said, straining against his ropes and drawing the attention momentarily away from Jack. He was not sure what the pirate was up to, but he was willing to help—if only to save himself.

Ignoring Will, Barbossa brought the discussion back around to the subject of profit. "I want fifty percent of your plunder," he told Jack.

"Twenty-five," countered Jack, "and I'll buy you the hat. The really big one . . . *Commodore*." Holding out his hand, he waited.

"Agreed," Barbossa finally said, as the room filled with the approving shouts of the crew. Turning his back on Jack and Will, Barbossa faced his men. It was time to procure himself the makings of a fleet.

"Gents," he shouted. "Take a walk."

From his spot right behind Barbossa, Jack cocked his head. A walk? But Norrington expected boats full of pirates.

Noticing Jack's confused expression, Barbossa smiled. Soon he would be a commodore, with Jack at his command, and not long after he would kill Will Turner and lift the curse. The night—and his future—was definitely growing brighter.

Outside the cave, the clouds parted, revealing the bright face of a full moon. The *Dauntless*, resting at anchor, was silent. Only a small crew of men was left to stand guard. Underneath the water, shafts of moonlight pierced the murky blue, illuminating a school of fish. Suddenly, the fish scattered in all directions as out of the shadows of the cave marched Barbossa's cursed crew.

Once again, their flesh had disappeared and only their bones could be seen through their tattered clothing. In their hands they held swords and pistols as they made their way toward the unsuspecting *Dauntless*. When they were directly beneath her hull they began to climb.

As the cursed pirates climbed aboard the *Dauntless*, Norrington and his men sat in the longboats, unaware of the impending danger facing their fellow crew members. All eyes were trained on the cave entrance, when they heard a splash and into view rowed a longboat. Inside the boat, sat Pintel and Ragetti, dressed in women's clothing. As Pintel rowed, Ragetti twirled a parasol about. "This is just like what the Greeks did at Troy," Ragetti said, smiling. "'cept they wore a horse n'stead of dresses." Rolling his eyes, Pintel continued to row.

Back aboard the *Dauntless*, Governor Swann made his way toward the captain's cabin. The day's events weighed heavily on his mind—especially Elizabeth's decision to wed. Knocking on the door, he waited for an answer from Elizabeth. When none came, he began to speak anyway. "I just want you to know . . . I couldn't be more proud of you," he said.

Inside the cabin, Elizabeth turned at the sound of her father's voice, but made no move to answer him or open the door. Instead, she continued to button up the red marine jacket she now wore. Finishing, she moved toward the window and looked down into the water below. At the ship's stern, a single longboat floated in the water, a long line of knotted sheets serving as a ladder to the boat. She had no intention of staying inside. Will was somewhere out there. Grabbing ahold of the rope, she began to climb down.

As Elizabeth rowed away into the shadows, Governor Swann finally stopped speaking. He found it odd that his daughter had not yet replied. Knocking once more, he opened the door. There was no one there! Rushing over, he glanced out the open window and saw the sheet ladder. Sighing, he looked out at the empty water.

Meanwhile, Pintel and Ragetti, still dressed as ladies, were rowing ever closer to the *Dauntless*. For a few confused moments, all eyes on the *Dauntless* were focused on the longboat, allowing the rest of Barbossa's crew to finish boarding the navy ship. Just as the last of the skeletons dropped onto the deck, Pintel and Ragetti floated into the moonlight, revealing their true identities. On the *Dauntless*'s helm, the commanding officer gasped and turning, his eyes grew wide. Climbing up the steps to the helm was a crew of skeletons! The marines rushed forward, their guns blasting and swords drawn, while out on the water Norrington heard the guns and ordered his men back to the ship. The *Dauntless* was under attack!

Below the helm, Governor Swann heard the commotion and raced over to the door, just in time to see a skeleton stab a marine through the chest. Slamming the door shut, he sunk to the floor, terrified.

As the battle raged on, Captain Jack Sparrow busied himself looking through the massive amounts of treasure that littered the cave. Off to one side, Will Turner stood glaring at the wily captain, while behind him Barbossa sat thinking. Unconcerned by Will's stares or Barbossa's ponderings, Jack lifted a gold statue, and held it up in the light.

"I must admit, Jack," Barbossa said thoughtfully. "You're a hard man to predict."

Turning to face Barbossa, the gold statue still in his hands, Jack raised his eyebrows.

"Me?" he asked, moving closer. "I'm dishonest. A dishonest man can always be trusted to be dishonest, honestly," he explained, tossing the statue over his head. Then, turning more toward Will, he added, "It's the honest ones you can't predict. You can never predict when they're going to do something incredibly . . . stupid."

As Jack explained himself, he moved closer and closer toward Twigg, one of the few pirates who had not gone out to the *Dauntless*. Suddenly, he reached down and grabbed the sword out of Twigg's belt and, with a kick, sent him flying into a puddle of seawater. Throwing the extra sword to Will, Jack pulled his own sword from its sheath and rushed Barbossa.

The sound of clashing iron filled the cave as the men fought, ducking in and out of the moonlight. Turning quickly, Will held out his hands, and Jack's sword slashed through the ropes that bound his wrists. Free, he turned to face his attackers. Seeing a skeleton where he expected a man, Will paused, but then quickly recovered and whipped his sword through the air.

Meanwhile, Jack and Barbossa parried across the cave, their swords flying furiously as each man tried to outdo the other. As their blades locked, Barbossa pulled Jack closer. "You're off the edge of the map, Jack," he said with a laugh. "Here there be monsters!"

With a cry, he pushed off, and the two men

continued fighting. Suddenly, Jack stepped to the side as Barbossa lunged forward and lost his balance. Taking advantage of the man's unguarded moment, Jack drove his sword through Barbossa's chest, pushing the captain back into a shaft of moonlight.

"You can't beat me, Jack," Barbossa said when he looked down and saw the hilt sticking out from his rib cage. In one swift move, he pulled the sword free and drove it back into Jack's chest.

For one long moment, there was silence as Jack looked down at his chest. Across the cave, Will paused midfight and looked over to see Jack stumble into the moonlight. As the light touched his skin, though, something happened. Instead of a body of flesh, Jack Sparrow was revealed to be a skeleton! He was cursed, too!

"Couldn't resist, mate," Jack said, pulling out the single gold coin he had taken from the chest and letting it clink over his skeletal fingers.

With a cry of rage, Barbossa lunged.

Chapter 24

Back out on the water, under the light of the full moon, Elizabeth rowed her boat up beside the *Black Pearl*. Pulling herself onto the empty deck, she pushed her long hair out of her face. She took a step forward and gasped as the skeleton monkey dropped down in front of her. A moment later, there was a clunk as the monkey fell overboard, landing on a cannon before it splashed into the water below.

On one of the decks below, two cursed pirates sat in front of a table covered in food. Looking from one treat to another, they tried to figure out what they would eat first when the curse was lifted. Hearing a splash, they looked out a cannon hole to the water below and then up to the deck just as Elizabeth looked down. With a cry, the pirates ducked back inside and headed up the stairs.

As the pirates went after Elizabeth, she

hurried down the stairs to the brig. There, still locked in a cell, was Jack's crew. Quickly, she raced over and let them out. If she was going to save Will, she would need all the help she could get.

Aboard the *Dauntless*, the fighting continued. Men and skeletons slashed at one another with swords, filling the air with the sounds of groans.

Governor Swann, meanwhile, was still hiding in the captain's cabin as the fighting outside raged. Suddenly, one of the skeleton pirates peered through the glass and caught sight of the cowering governor. Sticking his hand through the glass, he began to search for something to grab. Finally, his hand landed on the governor's wig, pulling it off. With a cry of rage, the governor grabbed the nearest thing he could find—a large candlestick—and brought it down on the pirate's arm. Looking down, he gasped. He was now holding the severed arm of a skeleton pirate—and it was still moving. Dropping it to the ground, the governor found himself being chased around the room by the disembodied hand. Finally, he leaned down, and grabbing the arm, shoved it into a drawer. Shaking, he leaned against the drawers, overwhelmed.

* * *

Back aboard the *Black Pearl*, Elizabeth Swann was trying to convince the ship's crew to join her in rescuing Will. Standing beside a single longboat, she looked up and down the line of pirates.

"Please," she begged, "I need your help!"

But her plea fell on deaf ears. Jack had promised the crew a ship and now they had one. Plus, there was the Code, as Gibbs pointed out.

"Hang the Code! They're more like guidelines anyway," she shouted, quoting Barbossa.

Moments later, she rowed toward *Isla de Muerta*—alone. Behind her, the *Pearl* began to pull away. "Bloody pirates," Elizabeth fumed.

While Elizabeth rowed toward the cave—and Will—Commodore Norrington and his men finally reached the *Dauntless*. Swords drawn, they leaped onto the deck and joined the fight. As swords clashed, Norrington shook his head in disbelief. A crew of skeletons? No one in Port Royal would believe this!

Captain Jack Sparrow was in quite the predicament—immortal or not. Back inside the cave, he and Barbossa battled, ducking in and out of the moonlight. Leaping atop a pile of gold, Jack's body turned skeletal as the light from the moon fell on him. A moment later, he jumped back down, pushing Barbossa against another pile of treasure. His sword pointed directly at the other captain, Jack smiled.

"So what now, Jack Sparrow," Barbossa sneered. "Are we to be two immortals, locked in epic battle till Judgment Day and the trumpets sound?"

Jack hesitated, thinking over the idea, before answering. "Or," he suggested, "you could surrender."

With a growl, Barbossa leaped forward and resumed the fight. There would be no surrender . . . not yet.

Meanwhile, across the cave, Will Turner continued to fight. As his sword slashed through the air, he found himself face-to-face with a pirate who went by the name of Jacoby. Suddenly, Will lost his footing and fell to the ground. Advancing upon him, sword drawn, Jacoby sneered. He would finish Will Turner off yet.

"I'll teach you the meaning of pain," he snarled.

"You like pain?" came a voice from behind Will. Looking over, Jacoby had only a moment to recognize Elizabeth Swann before she swung a heavy gaff across his face, knocking him to the ground. With a sneer, she added, "Try wearing a corset."

Satisfied that Jacoby was done with—for the moment—Elizabeth turned toward Will and offered him the other end of the gaff. Grabbing it, she hauled him to his feet. For a moment, the sound of swords clashing faded as the two looked into each other's eyes. Taking a step forward, Will smiled. But Elizabeth's attention was quickly drawn back to the fight at hand. Looking over, she watched as Barbossa and Jack slashed at each other, nothing more than skeletons in the moonlight.

"Whose side is Jack on?" Elizabeth asked, not at all surprised to see that Jack had taken on his old crew's curse.

Shrugging his shoulders, Will sighed. "At the moment . . ." he replied.

Nodding, Elizabeth turned. There was no time to figure out Jack Sparrow now. Leaving him to fight his own battles, she and Will lunged at a recovered Jacoby and two other cursed pirates. Elizabeth swung her gaff, hitting one of them square across the chest and knocking him into Jacoby. Working as a team, Elizabeth and Will continued to fight, keeping the three clustered together. Suddenly, seeing a chance to get the upper hand, they grabbed ahold of one end of the gaff and charged, lancing all three pirates together. Stepping back, they watched as the three looked down at the bar running through their chests. Then, smiling, Will picked up a bomb Jacoby had dropped and lit the fuse. Stepping forward, he shoved it inside the man's chest and with a nod to Elizabeth, they pushed the three men out of the moonlight and into a shadow.

Clutching at his chest, Jacoby looked up, smoke beginning to pour from his mouth. "No fair," he said. A moment later, the bomb exploded, blowing the undead pirates to smithereens.

Meanwhile, Jack and Barbossa were momentarily distracted by the sound of the explosion. Looking over, Jack watched as Will recovered his footing, and, grabbing the knife from atop the chest of Aztec Gold, he drew it across his palm. Quickly, Jack lashed out with his sword, catching the distracted Barbossa unaware. As the other captain struggled to stay upright, Jack threw his piece of the gold across the cave and watched as Will caught it in his hand.

At the same moment, Barbossa turned and pulled his pistol. Cocking it, he held out his arm and aimed—straight at the approaching Elizabeth. Seeing the gun pointed in her direction, she ground to a halt, almost losing her footing on the slippery rock beneath her feet. Across the cave, their eyes met as a shot rang out.

But it was not Barbossa's gun that had been fired. Perplexed, he turned and looked at Jack Sparrow, who stood, his smoking gun pointed directly at Barbossa's chest. "Ten years you carry that pistol, and now you waste your shot?" Barbossa said, a smile on his cracked lips.

"He didn't waste it," said Will.

Barbossa looked over to where Will stood, his left hand hovering above the Aztec chest. In his right hand Will held a knife, a strip of blood gleaming bright red in the moonlight. Barbossa watched in horror as Will opened his hand. Two pieces of gold—one the Medallion that Elizabeth had carried for so long and the other, Jack's piece—fell with a clink into the filled chest.

From where she stood, Elizabeth smiled as she watched Barbossa turn back to Jack, a look of anguish on his face. Looking down, Barbossa pulled aside his jacket and revealed his white shirt. Suddenly, a spot of red appeared and began to grow larger. Jack, gun still in hand, waited and watched as Barbossa began to grow pale.

"I feel cold," Barbossa said softly, before he fell back to the ground and, finally, died.

Back aboard the *Dauntless*, at the very same moment that Barbossa drew his last breath, Norrington and his men continued to fight. With a cry of rage, Norrington lunged, piercing the chest of one of the cursed pirates.

Shocked, the pirate looked down. From the

wound in his chest, blood began to flow, and as he fell, the other pirates looked down at their own bodies. In the bright light of the moon, their flesh was visible. They were no longer skeletons! The curse had been lifted!

And that meant they no longer had the upper hand.

One by one, they began to drop their weapons until they stood, unarmed, in front of the marines.

"The ship is *ours*, gentlemen," Norrington announced, and with a cry of victory, the marines thrust their swords into thc air.

Back inside *Isla de Muerta*, Elizabeth stood in front of a pile of gold, her eyes filled with sorrow. They had won. Barbossa had been defeated, and she had helped save Will. But the price had been high. When she left this cave, she would return to the *Dauntless* and become Norrington's fiancée. Feeling as though her heart were breaking, Elizabeth forced back tears.

Hearing footsteps, she turned and found herself looking into the eyes of the man she truly loved and now could never have—Will Turner.

Smiling tentatively, she waited for him to speak.

Will, his own heart racing as he gazed down at Elizabeth's face, did not know what to say. The promise had been made. She was to be Commodore Norrington's wife, and there was nothing he could do. He was a blacksmith's apprentice—he had nothing to offer. Opening his mouth to explain, he was silenced by a loud crash.

Looking over, both Elizabeth and Will watched as Captain Jack Sparrow sifted through various pieces of treasure, randomly throwing them over his shoulder.

"We should return to the *Dauntless*," Elizabeth said sadly.

Will nodded and braced himself. "Your fiancé will want to know you're safe," he said, trying to keep the bitterness out of his voice.

Elizabeth's eyes filled with tears as she nodded. Then she headed out of the cave. Walking up behind Will, a crown of gold on his head and his arms piled high with jewels, Jack watched Elizabeth retreat.

"If you were waiting for the opportune moment," he said, raising a finger in the air thoughtfully, "that was it." Then, as he continued past the heartbroken Will, he added, "Now, if you'd be so kind. I'd be much obliged if you could drop me at my ship."

Moments later, Jack sat at the prow of a longboat, looking out at the empty spot of sea where his ship was *supposed* to be. On his head he still wore the gold crown, and around his neck was a string of pearls.

"I'm sorry, Jack," Elizabeth said.

For a moment, the captain said nothing, only his eyes betraying his sadness. Then, with a sigh, he spoke. "They did what's right by them. Can't expect more than that."

Captain Jack Sparrow, who had defeated a cursed crew and saved a governor's daughter, found himself in an all-too-familiar position. He was, once again, a captain without a ship.

It was another beautiful day in the Caribbean. The sky was a brilliant shade of blue, and there was a faint breeze in the air. Suddenly, from high atop the cliff that overlooked Port Royal, the sound of drums filled the air. Glorious day or not, there was to be a hanging.

Standing in front of a noose, his hands tied in front of him, stood Captain Jack Sparrow. As he listened, an officer of the Royal Navy listed Jack's crimes. Hearing himself being referred to as "Jack Sparrow," Jack sighed and muttered, "Captain. It's *Captain* Jack Sparrow." Looking out over the crowd of people who had come to witness his hanging, Jack's gaze fell on a trio of familiar faces.

Decked out in their finest, Commodore Norrington, Elizabeth Swann, and Governor Swann stood on a platform a few steps above the crowd. Since they had arrived back in Port Royal,

Elizabeth had gone through the motions of being the commodore's fiancée. But that did not mean she agreed with his actions.

Staring at Jack Sparrow, she felt a horrible sense of loss. For better or worse, Jack had helped her and the man she truly loved. To see him die at the end of a noose seemed an affront.

"This is wrong," she said, speaking aloud.

Commodore Norrington heard the catch in her voice as she made her declaration. He was bound by law to hang pirates, and while he understood Elizabeth's sympathies—or at least allowed them—it did not change that. Jack Sparrow was to hang.

Suddenly, there was a shift in the crowd as someone began to make his way through. From their respective places, both Elizabeth and Jack strained to see who it was. A moment later, Will Turner appeared in front of Elizabeth. He wore a feathered cap, and resting on his shoulders was an elegant red cape. The combination was striking and when he spoke, his voice was bold.

"Elizabeth," he said, ignoring the glares of Norrington and the governor. "I should have told you—a long time ago. . . . I love you."

Elizabeth stood, shocked. She felt her heart begin to race. But before she could respond, Will nodded and disappeared into the crowd—just as the noose was placed around Jack's neck. Elizabeth glanced over and saw a familiar parrot land on a flagpole and caw. Smiling, she waited for what was to come. . . .

As he made his way through the crowd, Will pushed back his cape and revealed two swords that hung on either side of his belt. Pulling one out, he rushed toward the gallows, while behind him Elizabeth pretended to faint, distracting her father and the commodore momentarily.

Unfortunately for Jack, Will was one step behind the executioner. With a growl, the hooded man pulled a lever, sending Jack falling through a hole in the wooden floor. The rope tightened around his neck, but then, his flailing feet found something to rest on. Will's sword! Just as Jack had fallen, Will had managed to throw his sword, imbedding it deep into the wood below the gallow's hole, buying Jack precious moments. Leaping onto the gallows himself, Will pulled out his other sword and began to fight the executioner while Norrington and his men charged.

Back and forth, Will and the executioner fought—Will armed with a sword and the executioner a mighty ax. Suddenly, Will's sword was knocked from his hand and, ducking, he narrowly avoided being beheaded by the metal ax. However, the ax did not fail to hit the rope from which Jack hung, and with a creak it was severed, cutting Jack free. Beneath the gallows, Jack quickly ran his ropes over the sword still stuck in the wood and took off. A moment later, Will sent the executioner flying into the crowd as he too took off.

Safely away from the gallows, Jack took the other end of the rope that he had only moments ago been hanging from and threw it to Will. Together, the pair headed for the parapet side of Fort Charles, using the rope as a weapon as they went. Marines fell as the odd pair ducked and weaved, pulling the rope taut and knocking the men unconscious against the stone pillars that lined the fort.

But as the duo somersaulted out onto the ledge that lined the cliff, they suddenly realized that there was nowhere left to go. A moment later, they were surrounded by more than a dozen marines, cutlasses drawn. Spinning around, they looked for a way out, but it was too late. As Jack blew Will's hat feather out of his face, the commodore approached, sword drawn.

"I thought we would have to endure some manner of ill-conceived escape attempt," he said as he glared at Will. "But not from you."

Joining Norrington, Governor Swann looked at Will with disappointment. "When we returned, I granted you clemency," he said. "And this is how you thank me? By throwing in your lot with him? A pirate?"

"And a good man," Will said simply as behind him Jack nodded and pointed a finger at himself, as if to emphasize the point.

"You forget your place, Turner," Norrington responded.

But Will had not forgotten anything. His place was beside the man who had helped rescue Elizabeth and who had told him the truth about his father. And apparently, Elizabeth's place was beside Will. Pushing her way through the marines, she came to stand beside him, her hand resting on his arm and her chin high in defiance.

At the governor's order, the marines lowered their weapons. Watching Elizabeth gaze up at Will lovingly, Norrington sighed. "This is where your heart truly lies, then?" he asked at last.

"It is," she replied.

A flash of color drew Jack's attention away from the unfolding drama. Looking up, he grinned. Cotton's parrot! Sensing time was of the essence, Jack tiptoed around Will and Elizabeth and made his way over toward the commodore and the governor. "I'm actually feeling rather good about this," he said, bringing his face right up to the governor's. "I think we're all in a very special place—spiritually, ecumenically . . . grammatically." Sliding over to the commodore, he added, "I was rooting for you, mate. Know that."

Moving past a shocked and confused Elizabeth and Will, Jack jumped up onto the rim right below the fort's wall. Behind him, the cliff dropped steeply down into the crashing blue waves, while in front of him the marines stood at the ready, guns and swords drawn. Holding up a hand, Jack turned to the crowd. "Friends!" he said dramatically, "this is the day you will always remember as the day you *almost* . . ."

The rest of Jack's speech went unfinished as he tripped and fell back, plummeting head over feet into the water below.

Landing with a splash, Jack sputtered to the surface and gazed at the horizon. With a smile, his eyes landed on a familiar sight—the *Black Pearl*. Her black sails were no longer tattered and her sides gleamed in the bright sun. Grinning, Jack began to swim.

Back atop the cliff, Elizabeth and Will looked down at the water and then at each other. With a sigh, Will dragged his attention away from Elizabeth and looked over at Norrington. He had helped a pirate escape. Most likely, he now faced the hangman's noose.

But the commodore was not entirely without a heart. Drawing his sword, Norrington approached Will. "This is a beautiful sword," he said, holding up the same blade that had been given to him at his coronation ceremony not so long ago. "I expect the man who made it to show the same care and devotion to every aspect of his life."

Turning, he and the other officers moved off, but not before Norrington made it clear that

Jack Sparrow was not off the hook entirely—they would give him a day's head start.

Elizabeth and Will stood on the fort's parapet and gazed into each other's eyes. Governor Swann, seeing how happy his daughter was, sighed. It was not the life he had wanted for her, but she was headstrong and beyond his control. Just to be sure, he asked one last question, "So this is the path you've chosen? After all, he is a blacksmith."

Elizabeth looked over at her father and smiled. "No," she said proudly, turning back to Will and gently easing the hat off his head, "he's a pirate."

Leaning forward, Will pulled Elizabeth closer and there, high above the crystal blue waters, they melted into a long and lingering kiss.

Epilogue

Out at sea, Captain Jack Sparrow stood behind the wheel of the *Black Pearl.* On his head was the familiar tricornered hat and in his hand he held his Compass. As he looked out to sea and felt the *Black Pearl*'s wood beneath his fingers, Jack smiled.

"Now bring me that horizon," he said. And setting a new course, Captain Jack Sparrow sailed his ship across the turquoise waves of the Caribbean.